Praise for Lauren Dane's *Chased*

5 Ribbons   "The third book in Lauren Dane's CHASE BROTHERS series, CHASED, is a feisty read which I thoroughly enjoyed from beginning to end."

~ *Romance Junkies*

5 Lips   "Chased is the third book in the Chase Brothers Series by Lauren Dane. It is an intense story with a deep underlying theme of trust and sharing (...)I strongly urge everyone to read this book. You will not regret it."

~ *Two Lips Reviews*

5 Angels   "I absolutely, positively loved this book. It was sweet, funny and very hot. I really liked the way that Ms. Dane had the couple go slowly in their love. This was no-wham-bam-thank-you- ma-am kind of falling in love."

~ *Fallen Angel Reviews*

"CHASED by Lauren Dane continues her Chase Brothers series with another intriguing and titillating story that readers are certainly going to enjoy. I can't wait for Matt's story."

~ *Romance Reviews Today*

"CHASED is extraordinary. Completely different from the previous two installments of Ms. Dane's, Chase Brothers series, I found myself enthralled with Marc. A total ladies' man to the core, I was at first as unsure of him as Olivia. Charming to the core, his wooing of Liv was exquisite."

~ *Joyfully Reviewed*

"I loved it. I couldn't put Chased down, read it all in one sitting. Took less than a couple hours. That's usually my key indicator. This is another fantastic entry in the Chase brothers series."

~ *I Just Finished Reading*

4.5 nymphs   "Chased is the third book in the Chase Brothers series of books and just as fantastically fun as the two before it. Ms. Dane has created a great world for her Chase brothers and the women they fall head over heels for. Like riding in a speeding car, readers should be prepared for a fast and bumpy ride"

~ *Literary Nymphs*

4 Hearts   "This has been a terrific series thus far and CHASED adds another great layer of family drama and humor. Lauren Dane definitely stands out in contemporary romance as a shining star."

~ *The Romance Studio*

Chased

Lauren Dane

A SAMHAIN PUBLISHING, LTD. publication.

Samhain Publishing, Ltd.
512 Forest Lake Drive
Warner Robins, GA 31093
www.samhainpublishing.com

Chased
Copyright © 2007 by Lauren Dane
Print ISBN: 1-59998-631-0
Digital ISBN: 1-59998-436-9

Editing by Angie James
Cover by Scott Carpenter

First Samhain Publishing, Ltd. electronic publication: March 2007
First Samhain Publishing, Ltd. print publication: September 2007

Dedication

I'm often asked where I come up with my heroes. The honest truth is that there's a bit of my husband in every single hero I write. Loving, courageous, smart, loyal, passionate, strong, funny and sexy as all get out – he's my everything and he makes me whole.

And Angie, thanks for being blunt, taking no prisoners and whipping my words into shape.

As always, thank you to my beta readers who have a part in making each and every book better.

Chapter One

At the sound of the doorbell, Liv dabbed her eyes and cursed to herself, seeing they were still red and puffy. She'd have ignored it on any other day but Cassie and Maggie were picking her up to take her to drive over to Polly and Edward's fortieth wedding anniversary party.

Letting out a resigned sigh, Liv answered her door to her friends, both dressed to the nines.

"You've been crying." With a concerned look on her face, Maggie pushed her way into the house and Cassie followed.

"I'm fine. Really. I'm nearly done, I just need to fix my eyes. I don't want you two to be late."

"I've spent all afternoon with Polly, and Cassie took care of the set up. Edward's out with Polly, he's taking her for a drive. I think they're going to make out at the lake. And that means you're going to tell us what's going on." The look on Maggie's face told Liv she wouldn't back down.

"Brody." Liv sighed, turning to the mirror so she could repair her makeup.

"Brody what? What did he do?"

"Not what. Who. That rat bastard cheated on me with Lyndsay Cole. I walked in on them yesterday afternoon at his apartment. Got off work early and brought him some dinner. I got a lot more than the thank you I was expecting."

"He did not! She did not! That bitch," Maggie hissed. "That man-stealing bitch. I'm going to make a Lyndsay doll and stick her full of pins."

Liv snorted a laugh. "You always make me feel better. And someone was already sticking her full of something. But don't blame her. She wasn't in a relationship, Brody was. Pig."

"I hope his pecker falls off," Cassie said through clenched teeth.

"Or maybe it should get like a thousand paper cuts and then have lemon juice poured on it. And I hope Lyndsay gets a cold sore. A big one and a wart on her chin." Maggie nodded.

"With a big, black wiry hair that grows out of it and no one tells her," Cassie added.

"You two are the best." Liv grinned and turned around, finger combing her hair and smoothing down the front of the sweater dress she'd chosen for the party. "I feel better than I have since yesterday when I found out. I wish I could say he sucked in bed, but I'd be lying. What is it about me? Why can't I find someone? Something real?"

Maggie sighed. "You found out yesterday and you're only telling us now?"

Liv shrugged. "I couldn't face anyone. I caught them and I couldn't get it out of my head. You and Kyle had a date, Shane and Cassie only got back from their honeymoon and Dee and Arthur just finished the move to Atlanta. She's already got high blood pressure and I don't want to make her pregnancy worse. I came home, ate too much ice cream, watched *Thelma and Louise* and went to bed.

"I know Brody and I weren't engaged or anything. I didn't think he was the one, but I thought perhaps someday... Oh I don't know what I thought but I do know we were supposed to be exclusive. It could have been right some day to move to the next step. You know, he could have broken up with me. He didn't have to fuck someone behind my back."

Cassie hugged her tight and Maggie followed. "He's a pig. He's a pig, a jerk and a dick."

"And an ass. And his nose is big," Cassie added.

"Marc asked if I wanted him to kick Brody's ass." Liv grinned.

"You told Marc? You told Marc Chase before your best friend?" Maggie's eyebrows flew up.

"It just happened. He came by this afternoon looking for Shane. Something about the party. Anyway, he came by to look at my legs and flirt a bit and he asked if I was coming tonight with Brody and it just came out. He was very sweet about it."

Maggie harrumphed but looked mollified. "Well I suppose if you have to unburden such a shitty story to someone, it may as well be someone who looks as good as Marc does."

Liv laughed. "He does, doesn't he? Lawd, you should see the damned place every time he walks through, women coming out of the woodwork to be seen."

They all walked to the car and admittedly, Liv felt better.

"I just want someone I can trust. Someone I can come home to at the end of the day and share my life with. I want to be in love and get married and have kids. Not tomorrow or anything but I feel like I'm very far off schedule." Liv chewed her bottom lip as she pulled her seatbelt on.

"Love doesn't have a schedule, Liv." Maggie said from the back seat. "And you *will* find love. You will, I promise you. This thing with Brody isn't about you at all. He didn't cheat because you were bad. He cheated because he's a jerk."

"And Matt?" Liv's heart still ached a bit when she said his name.

"Matt is a good person, don't get me wrong. But he was not right for you. He's not right for anyone just yet. She'll come along though. But you aren't her and I'm sorry because I know you wish it was different. He's not ready."

"I want what you have with Kyle. What Cassie has. What Dee has. I look at Polly and Edward and think about how they've had forty years together and I wonder why I can't have that."

"You *can* have that. It'll come."

"It's only because you're pregnant that I don't smack you for saying that. People who are so happily married it makes my teeth hurt can say that stuff awfully easily. You have Kyle who looks at you like there's not another woman on Earth. Cassie has Shane who can't take his eyes off her for three minutes."

Maggie laughed. "No one but you two and Kyle knows about the pregnancy so watch it. Polly will kill me if she hears it before Kyle and I can tell her. As for you? Lotsa frogs in this world, Liv. Your prince is out there."

Liv groaned. "Maybe I need to sign up with a dating service or something."

Cassie shrugged. "I don't know, Liv. I mean, do those things work? Maybe you just need to get out there and meet people. Or give people a second chance. You're very picky. There are some great men in this town."

"Who are all married, cheaters or quite happily single like those damned Chase boys."

"Well, there's always Marc. He's damned good looking. Sweet too."

"Maggie Chase, Marc is way too young for me. Not to mention the fact that he goes through women like potato chips. I'm done being a potato chip."

"He is not too young for you. It's not like he's twenty or anything. But you're right about the potato chip part. Let's just look for someone appropriate then. In the meantime, you need to stop riding yourself so hard about this."

Easier said than done. Liv knew it wasn't a problem with her looks. Without vanity, she accepted that she was beautiful. The kind of woman who got second glances everywhere she went. She had a good job, a good life, she was intelligent and most people thought she was funny. She did have a bit of a smart mouth, but it wasn't like at nearly thirty-five she could change that part of herself. And she had self-respect, damn it. She would not start lying and biting her tongue just to appeal to men!

"You could always ask for Polly's help." Cassie winked as Liv groaned. "She's got her finger on the pulse of this town. She can find you an eligible man in minutes, I'd wager."

"You know, I may take her up on that if this goes on too much longer."

They pulled up out front and Liv sighed at the exterior of the house. Matt had strung white fairy lights in the trees out front and the lights inside burned out a warm, inviting glow. Truth be told, Liv missed being a regular part of the Chase family more than she missed Matt. Missed the house and Sunday dinners. Belonging to the Chase family had felt really wonderful.

"Ugh, I'm such a fucking whiner," she mumbled before joining Cassie and Maggie to go inside.

"By the way, nice tan." Liv put her arm around Cassie as they entered the foyer. "All that vacation sex really relaxed you."

Cassie laughed. "Shane, the sun, fruity drinks and lots of hot monkey love. I've never enjoyed myself more. Come on through, the present table is in the sitting room but we've set up the food in the back so that's where everyone will be."

"They're here!" Kyle yelled as Polly and Edward approached the door.

As Polly and Edward came into the house, everyone gathered shouted *Happy Anniversary!* Polly clapped her hands and started smooching up on everyone she could grab as Edward just took it all in with a calm smile.

They'd tried to plan a surprise party but Polly was too nosy and she'd found out early on. Instead, her sons and daughters-in-law had made Polly and Edward agree to let them plan the event and to stay out of the way until it was time to start.

Getting out of the way, Liv went to hang up her coat and bag before going back to the living room. She saw Polly Chase's hair first and then the rest of her as the crowd parted to let her through.

"Why hello there, Olivia. It's good to see you, honey. I'm glad you could make it." Polly click clacked on over in her stiletto heels, that giant, lacquered wall of hair not budging an inch as she moved.

Liv bent and hugged Polly, wishing her a happy anniversary. "I wouldn't miss it for the world. You and Edward are a fine example to the rest of us. I hope I can find what you two have someday."

"Aw, well, it's all Edward. The man is quiet, lets me have my way, doesn't say much. A good father and a good man. I'm fortunate." Polly turned and Liv followed her gaze to where Edward Chase stood with Matt.

It was hard to see him, even after a few years. There'd been a time when she'd believed Matt Chase was the one for her. He was attentive and fun, they had sexual chemistry that was off the charts and Liv kept thinking that soon he'd fall for her too. But it never happened. Sure, he had affection for her, but as they'd reached the year mark he hadn't moved even an inch toward marriage or living together. She'd tried to deny it, tried to pretend he'd change but in the end, she knew he didn't love her and never would.

Pride intact but heart broken, she'd left their relationship because it was time to go. She wanted something permanent and it wasn't fair to just spin her wheels with a man who'd never want more than a Saturday date.

Matt saw her and smiled. She waved in return.

"That boy is a fool." Polly shook her head and Liv warmed. "Tells me you're his best female friend. I said he doesn't need any more friends, he needs to settle down and if not with a beautiful, successful woman like you, who? I swear. Kyle was always the sweetest one so of course it wasn't a surprise when he ended up with Maggie. Shane, well, he's been a trial since the moment he was born but Cassie can handle him just fine. Marc doesn't think he needs forever but I think he needs it more than any of the others do. Matt though? I'm afraid he's going to be in for a rude awakening when he finally realizes just how much he let go when you left."

Fighting back tears, Liv squeezed Polly's hand. "Thank you for that, Mrs. Chase. That means a lot to me. He and I weren't meant to be. I wish that weren't so, but it is. And he is my best guy friend, even if he can be a total butthead. You raised four good boys. The last two will do fine when the right woman comes along."

"I'll have you know I have my eye out for a good man for you. I heard about that punk Brody Willitson from my Marc earlier today. Never liked him and he wasn't good enough for a girl like you, honey. Don't you worry though, I've got my ear to the ground." Polly winked. "Now get yourself a plate and have a drink, the night is young."

Liv watched, amused, as Polly ambled off to greet the next person who'd arrived when she saw Maggie with Marc.

"Hey, you two." Liv picked up a plate and began to fill it.

"Hey, Liv. I keep meaning to compliment you on that dress. Is that the one you bought online? That dark purple color is gorgeous on you." Maggie touched her arm.

"I have to agree with Maggie on that one, Liv. Now, as much as I like you in short skirts, this one is very nice. The appeal of a curve hugging sweater that's a dress is not lost on me at all. The boots are sexy too. A little bit dominatrix. You got any secrets to share, Livvy?"

Liv laughed to cover the warm surge in her belly that always came when Marc flirted. She knew he was full of it and flirted with every woman he met, but still, it made her feel tingly all over.

"Have you seen the bench we got them?" Marc held his arm out and Liv took it, letting him lead her out of the room, through the kitchen and out into the large backyard.

"Kyle landscaped this little alcove for it. He says the roses will bloom over the arbor in the summer and night blooming jasmine is planted on both sides."

The bench sat in an isolated corner of the yard with a pretty white arbor over it and a fountain nearby.

"Momma saw the bench last year during the insanity after Christmas when they were planning the wedding and Cassie told Shane and it went from there. You see the plaque?"

On the back of the bench, an inscribed plaque with Polly and Edward's name and anniversary date.

"It's impossible to shop for them but this and the album of all the pictures we had made from the slides my daddy had have been the biggest hit yet." Marc sat down and Liv joined him.

Liv warmed at the affection in his voice. "It's really beautiful out here. Kyle did a great job at making this little place. Like an oasis for the two of them to come and sit together."

"He'll read and pretend to listen to her and she'll talk and cross-stitch and pretend he's listening when she's really just planning on getting me and Matt married off."

Liv laughed out loud at the truth of that statement. "They work."

"They do. One day, if I can have what they do, even a shadow of what they have, I'll be lucky."

Liv nodded as she picked at the food on her plate and Marc helped himself to it as well. The noise from the party wafted out on the air but their corner of the yard was an isolated haven. They didn't talk, instead just looked at the stars and picked at Liv's food.

"We should probably go back inside," Liv said, standing. She needed to get back inside before she gave in and leaned her head on his shoulder.

"Yeah, it'll be cake time soon. I love cake." He pressed a quick kiss to her cheek. "Don't forget that you owe me a dance later."

"We'll see."

"No seeing about it, Olivia Davis. You owe me a dance and I mean to collect." Popping a stolen olive into his mouth, he drew her back into the house, letting her go ahead once they reached the porch.

Man-oh-man did he love to look at her. Tall, long legs, big brown eyes that always looked like she had a very naughty secret and hair as black as a raven's wing. Straight and glossy and usually in some short, stylish 'do. Her clothes, just shy of outright sexy but it was clear she was a woman who knew what looked good on her body and she dressed accordingly. Not too tight but certainly clingy enough to highlight the high, round ass and the legs. She wore heels high enough to show off hard calves and tilted her ass and breasts out just right. The blouses and sweaters lovingly showcased her perky B cups.

He adored her smile. One of those smiles women had when they knew something delicious. Her accent was nice and thick—sexy, soft southern sin—and she always sounded on the verge of laughing.

Liv Davis was just an all around package. Funny, intelligent, independent, very feminine but capable too. She never ceased to make him smile when he thought about her. And she was the only woman he knew who flirted as well as he did. He had to admire that.

Once they got back inside, Liv got pulled into a cutthroat game of canasta with Marc, Cassie and Shane.

"Sheesh, I was hoping your mind would still be addled with all that honeymoon nookie but you're a shark with the cards," Liv joked with Cassie.

"I don't play to lose, Liv." Cassie sniffed and tossed down some cards, reaching to draw more.

"I love it when you're vicious, beautiful," Shane said and Marc rolled his eyes.

"Stop before it starts. No cow eyes over the cards. Chase family rule."

Liv laughed. "I like that rule."

"I hear the music starting up in the other room, Olivia. You promised me a dance don't you forget." Marc winked.

"Let me just do this." Liv tossed down her last suit and stood with a smile. "I don't play to lose either."

Cassie laughed and Marc stood. "Okay then, darlin', let's dance."

Liv took his hand and let him lead her through the house to the formal living room where the music was playing.

With an artful flourish, he pulled her into his arms and against his body. They both froze a moment and moved a bit apart. Swaying slowly, they chatted about town gossip as Reba sang over the stereo speakers.

That night when she finally got home, sore feet and all, the small of her back still tingled where his hand laid when they'd shared a dance. "I must be ten kinds of fool for even entertaining the thought," she mumbled to herself as she tossed and turned.

But her dreams had other ideas.

Chapter Two

Marc happened to find himself standing in the front window of The Sands looking through the glass at Liv Davis as she reached out and touched the cheek of another man. The affection in her eyes startled him. He would have felt jealous but the man was clearly thirty years older than she was and the touch wasn't sexual at all. There was something else there he hadn't seen with Liv before, a sort of yearning.

When she looked up and saw him, surprise won over her face followed by a smile. There was nothing else he could do but go inside after she looked at him that way.

"Hi there, sugar." He strolled up to her table.

"Hi Marc. Listen, I want you to meet my dad. He's visiting my sister in Atlanta for a week or so and came out to see me as well. Dad, this is Marc Chase. Marc, this is my father Bill Davis."

Marc shook the other man's hand. "It's a pleasure to meet you, Mr. Davis. Liv has spoken of you often. How's life in Florida treating you?"

"Sit down, boy." Bill Davis gestured to the place next to Liv, and Marc liked the man even more as he sat. "Florida is good, my lungs are much happier now, although I miss my baby girls. I was just trying to convince Livvy here to move down to be near me."

Marc didn't like the feeling in his stomach at the thought of that desk in the mayor's office being filled by someone else.

"But what would we do without her, Mr. Davis? Maggie might expect me to listen to all that girl talk if Liv wasn't around."

Liv snorted. "If I moved down there all his little girlfriends would be put out. He's the king of his senior community. He thinks he wants me and my sister there but he's got a harem to take care of him and they'll put up with a lot more than we will."

Marc stayed for pie and had to get moving. He had a meeting at the bank about a small business loan. But as he sat waiting to speak to the loan manager, his mind kept returning to the night of the anniversary party. It'd felt good with his body against hers, his hand at the curve of her back, holding her there, warm and soft, the scent of her in his nose. The itch to taste her rode him hard, he'd wanted to kiss her pretty bad but his father had cut in, stopping him before he did it.

It wasn't like he hadn't thought of asking Liv out before. At first she was freshly broken up with Matt and it was too soon. But the year mark had long passed and he'd brought it up to her and she'd deflected it. She didn't seem to take him or his advances seriously and he'd never really tried to make it more clear.

They called him into the meeting and he cleared his mind and got it back on business. In the end, the papers were relatively simple and Marc signed on the bottom line, in triplicate, and took out a loan he tried not to think about the size of. Some minutes later a few blocks away, he signed the lease on a space that would hold his gym and where he'd also run his personal training business from.

"When do you need me to help paint?" Kyle asked from the doorway.

Marc turned to face his brother. "Don't offer if you don't mean it. I'll put your butt to work."

"Of course I mean it. This is your dream, Marc. I'm your brother. You helped me on weekends how many times when I was getting the landscaping business up and running? That's what family does." Kyle came into the space. "This is a good spot. Central. Good lighting."

"This your place now?"

"Hey, Matt." Marc waved and his heart warmed to see Shane darken the doorway as he followed Matt.

"Well, now. This place is nice." Shane looked around the room.

"The paint is waiting at Pete's to pick up. The mirrors are ready. The floor people delivered the supplies to Pete's as well. I took off all next week." Marc walked around, envisioning just where he'd put everything. It wouldn't be a large gym but focused on the personal needs of not more than ten people working out at once. The space had been a gym some years ago so there were already two dressing rooms in the back with showers and lockers. He didn't plan on a juice bar or water aerobics. His place would be simple. But he would work with others to refer out as needed. He could help his clients with nutritional counseling but he'd been in contact with a woman in town to help with cooking classes or even meal delivery for his clients on an as needed basis.

"Okay, we'll strip the walls before we get the flooring down. Get the paint up, the mirrors in and then do the floors. Where's the equipment?" Shane, ever the organizer, made Marc smile.

"Murph is letting me store it there until I'm ready."

"When's your last day at Murphy's?"

Murphy's was the gym in Riverton that he'd worked at for the last five years as a personal trainer.

"The end of the month."

"Well, tomorrow is Saturday, let's get in here first thing and get these walls cleaned up. You're coming to Momma and Daddy's before The Pumphouse tonight, right?" Kyle asked.

"I wouldn't miss this announcement for the world. Should I act surprised when Maggie tells us all she's knocked up?" Marc grinned.

"How'd you know?"

"Kyle." Matt rolled his eyes. "What other sort of big announcement is there? And she's been pretty green on and off over the last two months. She hasn't had a beer that I've seen since before Christmas and she's got a tiny little bump in her belly."

"And her boobs are bigger," Marc added.

"Thank you for that, Marc. So much tact." Shane chuckled. "Congratulations, Kyle. We figured you'd tell us when you were ready. After the miscarriage, we knew you'd want to wait to tell people this time. Although I'm absolutely sure Cassie knows but hasn't said."

Kyle laughed. "Count on it. I wasn't allowed to tell anyone but I know darned well Maggie told Cassie and Liv. Those three are thick as thieves. I was sorry to see Dee and Arthur move to Atlanta, I know Maggie misses her sorely."

"Yeah. Things are changing. You're gonna be a daddy. Shane is married and not grumpy all the time. Matt, well Matt is still Matt but you know what I mean."

"I know I saw you looking at Liv last night like she was a steak and you were a starving man," Matt said to Marc, eyeing him closely.

"That so? And if I did?" Marc wasn't sure if he felt defensive or not. He didn't feel embarrassed though.

Matt sighed. "What's your game? I may have messed things up with her, but she's one of my best friends and I don't want her hurt. After this mess with Brody, she doesn't need some guy who only wants a one night stand."

"Look, Matt, you're my brother so I'm gonna let that insult slide. I like Olivia. She's gorgeous on the outside but I like her insides too. I want to be her friend. I *am* her friend. I'm not an asshole."

"I'm not insulting you. But she's not a notch on your bedpost."

"And that's not an insult?" Marc's voice rose and Kyle stepped in between them both.

"Whoa. That's enough. Matt, you're being insulting. Marc isn't some slutty user. Have you ever seen one single woman in this town hate him? I've never seen him less than respectful to a woman. And Marc, Matt is just trying to say that if you're not looking for something long term to not start anything with Liv." Kyle put a hand on each of their shoulders. "You two are brothers. Stop it now."

Shane grinned. "You're good at that, Kyle. If you ever get tired of landscaping, you should be a counselor. And, Marc, for the record, I think a woman like Liv is exactly what you need. I'm not trying to convert you to the ways of a married man but I do think it's time you started thinking about being with a woman for longer than a few weeks at a time."

"I'm sorry if I offended you, Marc." Matt patted Marc's shoulder.

"Me too. Let's go to Momma and Daddy's and listen to the squeals of delight before we go play some pool."

࿊࿊࿊

Marc played pool and thought about the whole night. From the elation of finally carving out something for himself to the joy of Kyle and Maggie's announcement.

He'd been the baby of the family, living in the shadow of the other men in his life. His father, an upstanding pillar of the community. His oldest brother who'd always been the kind of guy you could trust to get your back. Upstanding, intense, loyal to his family. Kyle, good hearted, hard working small business owner, a wonder with the ladies until Maggie came along and now a devoted husband and soon-to-be parent. Matt, who liked to pretend he was just an affable, lazy guy but who excelled at everything he'd ever done. Perfect grades in school, highest scores when he went to the academy and well liked and respected at the firehouse.

It was hard to find your identity when your brothers were all such fine men. And he'd been content enough working at Murphy's, but over the last two years, he'd realized just how much he liked being a personal trainer. He wanted something of his own and closer to home. He wanted to help people live healthier lives in his community.

Maybe it was time for some more changes in his life.

He watched Liv and thought some more. Wondered if the longevity of her appeal to him was a matter of her unavailability or whether she was someone he could actually have a relationship with.

There was really only one way to find out.

࿊࿊࿊

"So uh, when did you and Marc start looking at each other like you were imagining each other naked?" Cassie asked as she drank her beer.

Liv started. "What?"

Maggie just raised an eyebrow and Liv sighed. "Okay. Okay. I don't know. I've always thought he was handsome. It's just flirting. Don't go picking out china patterns for me. He's way too young and as I said before, he's not looking for anything serious or long term and I'm done with men who aren't. I may look and he may look but that's all it is. Looking."

"And I said he's not too young. He's what? Six years younger? That's not a thing. Men go out with women ten, fifteen years younger all the time. And I share a bedroom with the former wiliest bachelor in all the county. Apparently when these Chase boys decide to settle down, they do it for real." Cassie shrugged.

"You've seen Marc right? He's really hot. He works in a gym, his body is off the chain. He's got the most beautiful green eyes and I love that his hair is the darkest of all the boys. Nice, sort of just rolled out of bed features too. Of course I'm gonna look. Sheesh. A woman would have to be dead not to look. But that's all there is to it. Now, moving along to another topic. How did the announcement go?"

"As predicted. Polly is probably out buying furniture for the nursery right now. She insisted that they have a room for the baby at their house for when they babysit and so she or he will have a comfortable place to sleep when we're having dinner there or whatnot."

Cassie burst out laughing. "Yeah, like that baby will be put down in a crib with Polly around. I'm glad you're doing it first. Between Polly, Edward and those boys, you're never going to be able to hold your own baby."

"I'm happy for you. You and Kyle are going to be such great parents." Liv smiled.

"And you two will be the best aunties a baby could ever wish for."

"Free babysitting for life. What girl could ask for more?" Liv winked. "So when do we start the childbirth classes?"

Maggie laughed. "We've got a few months. I'm gonna need you to take a heavy hand to keep the delivery room clear."

"You got it, ace, I'll be your hired muscle." Her best friend and the person she loved most in the world was having a baby. Wow. They were all growing up and life was changing.

A pang sliced through Liv as she wondered when and if she'd be having a baby with a man who adored her as much as Kyle did Maggie. No one had ever looked at her that way, with such love and adoration, she had no real frame of reference at being cherished.

৪৩৪৩৫৪৩

Marc looked down from his place on the ladder to see Olivia walk in.

"Hey there. What brings such a beautiful lady into my gym on such a nice day?"

She looked up and they locked gazes a moment. "You're just a jack-of-all-trades, aren't you? You're an electrician too?"

"Oh this is pretty simple stuff. The lights look better when they're set into the ceiling instead of hanging, I think." Finishing up, he came back down and put his toolbox aside. "What can I do for you?"

"Do you have room for another client? I've been feeling winded and out of shape doing simple stuff and it's harder for me to maintain my weight than it used to be. So I figure I could use your help."

And she was helping keep his business afloat too. He warmed, thinking about her wanting to help him out.

"I don't see an ounce of fat on you. And I think I've looked closely enough." He winked and she laughed. "Well let's sit down and talk about your goals and what you're looking to do with yourself."

He interviewed her and got a better idea of the kind of services she'd need from him.

"I'm not going to let you slack, you know. I'm a tough taskmaster."

"And I'm not some weak little girl either. I can take it and my ass and upper arms need it."

Craning his neck, Marc checked out the area in question. "Honey, your ass is just perfect. Do you want to work out here or at your place?"

"I don't have the equipment at home so I guess here."

"Well, let's get some measurements then." He stood and indicated the scales.

"Do I have to?" She blanched.

"I don't know why women are always so freaked by the scale. It's just one indicator and it doesn't mean anything at this stage. You have nothing to worry about. Now come on."

"Should I take my shoes off?"

"Do you want to? It's not going to make much of a difference you know. If it makes you feel better, you go on. I bet you have pretty toes anyway."

Marc was very matter-of-fact when he worked with clients. He didn't coddle or pump up egos for no reason. He gave praise when it was due, and criticism in a constructive manner.

She sighed and stepped on the scale. With her shoes on. He liked her grit.

"You're well within normal weight range for your height." He took a body fat measurement and then brought out a tape measure to get her arms, legs, waist, hips and chest. Taking all the numbers down.

He discussed targets with her and they set up a schedule.

"I'll give you the family discount," he said, reaching for her credit card. "If you're not satisfied at the end of one month, I'll give you a fifty percent refund. But you have to work at it."

"You are not giving me a discount. You just started your own business. Later, when you're a mogul here in Petal you can give me a discount. And I told you, I'm not afraid of hard work."

"I like the set of your mouth when you get uppity." He gave her the family discount anyway and watched her as she walked out the door and to her car. He jogged to the door.

"Hey!"

She turned and waited.

"Walk tomorrow. You have enough time to get home from work and change out of your clothes. Walk and it'll be a nice warm up."

He couldn't help but love the way her eyes narrowed at him and her hand cocked on her hip. But she only nodded and got in her car, and he laughed as she pulled away.

"Feisty."

ಬಂಬಂಡಿ

As promised, she showed up the next night—on foot. The walk wasn't that far and she found that the time enabled her to get rid of her day and begin to focus on working out for herself.

"Good evenin', Olivia." Marc handed her a key. "This is for the locker in the dressing room. You can stow your stuff in there. Come on out and we'll get started."

There were two other people working on the machines when she emerged from the dressing room. He'd said that there would be other people working out when she was there but he'd be available to her one-on-one when she needed it. Apparently, there were just simple gym members and those who needed less than a one-on-one trainer. She liked seeing his business getting off to a good start. Wanted things to work for him.

He went through the weights with her. Showed her the proper way to lift the weights and to extend her muscles. Instructed her on each machine and made notes in her personal log about her stamina. Which embarrassed her. She was used to being good at things, but she was out of shape and pretty darned sweaty and tired by the time she was done.

But she'd be damned if she let that get to her. No, she'd work her ass off to get it in shape because she said she would. And anyway, it would keep her from obsessing about her lack of a love life.

Of course, it did help that he looked so darned good. It was easy to mentally wander off to her happy place while her muscles screamed for mercy. For his part, he hadn't flirted at all, had kept his behavior professionally genial. Still though, he smelled good and when he leaned over her to adjust the weights on what she thought of as the thigh buster, she wanted to take a bite out of him.

"You're done for tonight. This will be your workout on Mondays and Fridays. Wednesdays and Saturdays you'll do aerobic exercise. We'll go for a run on Wednesday morning before work as planned and Saturdays I've got a bike ride set up for my clients who are interested. This week I thought the lake trail would be good. I can get an idea of where you're all at stamina wise. And then I'll set up individual appointments with you as necessary. Have you ever tried kickboxing or rowing?"

She just stared at him for long moments until he laughed. "What?"

"Nothing. I've just realized I'm paying you to kill me."

"You're paying me to extend your life, Olivia. Now go on. I'll see you Wednesday morning at six. I'll swing by your place to pick you up. You okay to walk home?"

"It's five blocks. People are still out and about and it's Petal." She softened a bit. "But thank you, I appreciate your asking."

"Okay then. Take it slow, don't dawdle but let your muscles cool down."

Liv had the foolish need to kiss him goodbye but a new client came in. A female one who giggled at him. Gnashing her teeth, Liv remembered herself, pokered up and waved quickly before leaving.

As she walked home, she gave herself a stern talking to about this new infatuation with Marc Chase. She needed to keep in mind who Marc was. No, *what* Marc was. A very nice, very flirty guy. She wasn't anything more than another woman to wink at. A woman six years older than he was. She wasn't Mrs. Robinson and he wasn't what she was looking for, even if he was interested in her romantically, which he wasn't.

It was a fun, flirty friendship. Period. End of sentence. She'd be a fool to entertain anything other than that. And Liv Davis may be staring spinsterhood in the face but she was not a fool.

Chapter Three

Liv sat eating her lunch at The Sands, looking out onto Main Street. It was a Wednesday, she'd had a good run that morning with Marc. Even though it had been a month and he didn't need to run with her every week any more, he still did, said it kept him healthy too.

Wasn't like she was going to complain. She liked hanging out with him. When she'd been going out with Matt, Marc was the saucy little brother. She knew him but only as someone to say hello to on the street and to talk to about shallow topics at Sunday dinner.

She never got to actually know the Marc Chase who cared deeply about physical fitness and nutrition. The Marc who was a lot deeper than she'd given him credit for.

"Are those potato chips on your plate?"

Speak of the devil. Liv looked up into those gorgeous green eyes and blushed. "Yes. Baked, not fried. I swear. And I asked for half an order. No mayo on the sandwich and you can see it's nine grain bread."

Laughing he slid into the booth across from her. "Good job. Trans fats are the worst. And anyway, if you use all your calories up on crap, you can't have smothered pork chops for Sunday dinner."

That was another thing. He cared about eating right and living healthy but not in a fanatical sense. He enjoyed life and wanted his clients to as well.

"I save my weekly splurge for Friday nights at The Pumphouse."

He laughed. "I have to do extra time on the rowing machine for chili cheese fries."

She only barely managed to bite back a comment about how good his stomach looked as he used the rowing machine. Flex and release, flex and release, the muscles in his abdomen were hard and toned and she squirmed a little in her seat as she thought about it.

"Can I join you? I haven't had lunch yet."

She nodded and he ordered. There was something about him that made her feel relaxed. Well, stuff about him that made her feel nervous and edgy too but that was the lack of sex. It had been six weeks since she'd had sex and she felt like she was going insane with the stress. And the marvelous hunk of man cake in front of her just ached to be licked from head to toe.

A giggle bubbled up before she could stop it. The lack of sex really was driving her mad.

"What's so funny?" Marc's smile was infectious and she laughed again.

"Nothing. Just a silly thought I had that I'm *not* going to share."

"Ah. A sex thought. About me I bet. I know I have plenty about you. I can say that since we're not working now," he added.

"You're incorrigible. I'm old enough to be your, um, babysitter."

"Trust me, Olivia. Momma left us with a few babysitters here and there, not very often, you know, because they never came back after the first time. But none of them looked like you. We might have behaved if they did."

"Oh you guys. Did you torture a bunch of teenaged girls? Setting fires and egging cars?"

"We never set fires."

Liv began laughing anew at the thought of the four Chase boys terrorizing their babysitters.

"It was all Shane. I just followed along. I'm totally innocent." He put his hands up, struggling against a laugh.

"Oh no more. I'm going to choke on something," she gasped out through the laughter. "You innocent?"

Marc realized as they laughed together that something really essential had passed between them. Had changed. She wasn't Matt's ex-girlfriend anymore. She was his friend. Totally separate from her former relationship with his brother. Free from that. What they had was unique to the two of them and it all sort of clicked into place.

"Okay, so innocent probably isn't the best word choice. But Shane is an instigator. He may be the sheriff now but it's only because he was such a lawbreaker when we were kids. Oh, Daddy used to get so mad. And my dad rarely gets riled up. Momma, well she'd grab for whatever son she could grab a hank of and hold on to, screeching the whole time. Once she had your ear, you were done with, and you may as well just submit or she'd never let you go. But Daddy? He'd bide his time until we all thought the coast was clear and then he'd corner us in his study or the kitchen and man we'd get it." He smiled at the memory.

"Your mother is something else. I love her to death but she scares the hell out of me."

"I'd say she was all bark and no bite but that'd be such a lie. She's fierce for such a tiny scrap of woman. Taught me a lot about courage. My father taught me about justice and honor but Momma taught me courage and tenacity." Marc wondered what she'd think about him and Liv and realized the moment he thought it that his mother would be all for it. Liv had already passed inspection and been approved. It was Matt who fucked up.

"I love the way she terrorizes John. The mayor that is. This whole Founder's Day event has been fun to plan but every time she enters the building he tries to jump out his office window. He tries to charm his way around her but she sees right through him and he just gives in with a heavy sigh."

Marc didn't like the first name thing. Wondered if she had a thing with the mayor and then discarded the idea. John Woodward was not the kind of man who could hold a woman like Olivia Davis for longer than three minutes. He certainly couldn't match her in bed. John was too timid and gentlemanly. Marc knew what Liv needed between the sheets. Passion. Energy. Creativity and if he wasn't wrong, a bit of a dominant hand.

"You going then? To the picnic and parade?" Marc asked, he hoped not too eagerly.

"Wouldn't miss it. Should be a big shindig and your mother has worked really hard with the historical society. And I love a good party." She crumpled her napkin and grabbed her bag. "I need to get back to work. It was nice to hang out with you today." She put a hand on his shoulder to stay him. "Don't get up. I'll see you later, Marc. Have a nice afternoon."

"I'll see you Friday," he called out, relieved his voice hadn't cracked at the weight of awareness of her as a woman. Holy moley, he wanted her bad. Seeing her laugh like that, her head tipped back slightly so her neck was exposed, all creamy and supple made him want to lick all the way from shoulder to earlobe. Wondered if she would give a little shiver of delight. Wondered what she'd taste like.

Groaning, he put his forehead in his palm. This couldn't be happening to him. He was not going down like his older brothers had. No way. But he would taste Olivia Davis. To get her out of his system, of course. Once they'd had each other a few dozen times the desperate need he felt would wear off. Yeah. That was it.

ॐॐॐ

Torture. That's what it was and she had to end it. Liv looked at Marc Chase as he sat on a blanket with Becky Sue Radin. The teeny little blonde stared at him like he was a cupcake. And Liv loved cupcakes too, but since Marc hired on as her personal trainer she hadn't had one. That was clearly her problem. A lack of cupcakes. It was all Marc's fault. Cupcake deprivation had led her into sexualizing everything.

Huffing out a breath in frustration, she turned her attention back to Bill Prentiss, who'd been telling her all about his prize winning steer. *Fascinating.* Okay, she was being unfair. Bill was a perfectly nice man. Owned a ranch outside town. Made a good living. Worked hard and was quite a handsome specimen. Marriage material even.

He held her hand gently, respectfully and paid attention to no other woman but her. These were *good things* and if she wanted forever, she'd have to stop this ridiculous attraction to men like Marc and Matt Chase, who didn't think ten minutes ahead of their little misters.

No, Liv Davis was done with the sweet talking ladies' men of the world. They might be fun as all get out between the sheets but there was more to life than between the sheets.

So she smiled at Bill and flattered him because he deserved it. It was all *her* issue that she had some kind of messed up gene that found unworthy men attractive. She had to stamp it out. Retrain herself. Yes. That's exactly what she needed to do. Retrain herself.

"Bill, I'll be back in a few minutes. I just need to check in on the ladies around the corner to be sure they've got enough ice and everything they need."

He stood when she did and she cocked her head, smiling. He really was a nice man and she'd be a fool not to go out with him again if he asked.

"I'll be right here, Liv. Unless there's something I can do to help?"

"That's very kind of you but, no thank you. I just promised the mayor that I'd be on the lookout in case the historical society ladies needed anything. Back in a bit."

Of course, as she'd figured, Polly Chase didn't need a thing. She had the entire evening planned to perfection, including the pie booth. Polly thanked Liv, pressed a peach popover on her and Liv headed into the building to get a sweater out of her office as the evening had gotten a bit chilly.

"Hey there. Whatcha doing in here?"

She nearly jumped out of her skin when Marc spoke behind her as she left the building on the side away from the crowds. "Jeez, give a girl a heart attack!"

"Sorry. I ran to my truck to grab a blanket. It's getting a bit cold. Should have known. It is mid-April."

He made no move to leave though. Standing there, staring at her mouth in the moonlight.

"Do I have sugar on my lips?" She felt slightly guilty for eating the popover and made a promise to herself to go and grab Bill a piece of something sweet.

He stepped forward and she had no place to go, the wall was at her back. "I don't know. Do you?" he murmured, his body just shy of touching hers.

"I...uh." Before she could say anything else so spectacularly witty, he closed the last inch between them, his hand moving to cup her cheek.

"You're one of the most beautiful women I've ever seen. I've always thought so. Soft. You smell good too."

"Marc..."

His lips brushed hers, just the barest hint of pressure but within a breath, that soft touch exploded and need so dire it scared her, welled up and swallowed her whole.

It must have been the same for him because he angled his mouth and went in for a real kiss this time. A skillful combination of teeth, tongue and lips all working to devastate her defenses. Her fingers gripped his shoulders, digging into the muscles, registering the softness of the sweater he was wearing.

His taste bloomed through her, spicy, delicious. It made something deep within her ache for a moment, seize and then warm all over. A soft moan escaped her and he swallowed it eagerly.

His hands, large and capable, held her hips, the tips of his thumbs stroking over the naked skin just beneath the hem of her sweater, just two inches shy of the bottom slope of her breasts.

That's what snapped her out of it, the longing, the yearning to reach down and move his hands up over her breasts and arch into his touch. She let go of his shoulders, sliding her palms down to push him back gently.

"Holy moley," Marc breathed out.

She nodded.

"When can you leave? We can go get a late drink somewhere or you could come to my place." Marc brushed a thumb over her bottom lip and she shivered.

"I'm here on a date, Marc. God, I shouldn't have done that." Especially because it awakened something deep inside her, a recognition that freaked her out. It was something she couldn't afford to feel. He wasn't capable of giving it back.

"Of course you should have. Olivia, this thing, that kiss has been brewing between the two of us for a long time now and you know it. We can go to dinner another night. I'm sorry for suggesting you dump your date. I know you're too kind to do that."

"I can't have dinner with you, Marc. Not tonight, not tomorrow night."

"Okay, well then come to my apartment. I'll make you dinner after I've had you three or four times." He grinned and she groaned, pushing him back so she could move away from the wall. She felt cornered in more ways than one. She vowed to eat a cupcake that very night. Two even. This addiction to dangerously handsome men without an ounce of desire to commit would be the death of her.

"There'll be no having!"

"Oh now, Olivia, don't be offended. I didn't mean it to sound crass."

She shoved a hand through her hair. "No, not that. I'm not offended. I'm flattered. Confused." Panicked, scared, freaked, aroused and a dozen other things it would not pay to feel. "But it can't happen, Marc. Not ever."

He narrowed his eyes at her. "You're joking. Olivia Davis, that was the single most hottest kiss I've ever shared with a woman and you were on fire in my arms. I felt your nipples through your sweater. You wanted me, you can't deny that."

Oy. "I'm not denying that. Yes, yes there's chemistry but there are too many reasons to not give in."

He put his hands on his hips. "Like what? You're single, I'm single. We're attracted to each other and you know we're going to be hot in bed together."

"Marc, you're too young for me. I'm six years older than you are. And," she held up her hand to silence him, "I've just recently decided that I'm done with casual relationships. I am not going out with another man who thinks of women as a box of chocolates and he has to sample every one. I want something real, something lasting and that's not what you want. I'm not judging you, Marc, but I want a relationship. I want to end up married."

He paled so much she could see it in the moonlight. She laughed tightly. She'd known it but it hurt to see his reaction anyway.

"See? Even the word freaks you out. You and I are friends. We really are and I like that. I like *you*. But this can't be more than a friendship, spectacular kiss or not. Now I have a date who'll be wondering where I am and you do too if I'm not mistaken. I'll see you on Monday when I come to work out."

She hurried off before she changed her mind.

Watching her walk away, Marc slammed his fist into his thigh in frustration. *Friends?* After that kiss? His lips tingled

38

with her taste, his cock throbbed, pressing against the fly of his jeans.

"Too young my ass," he mumbled, heading back to where Becky Sue waited for him. It wasn't like Liv was old. She was gorgeous and totally in shape. He knew that for sure. He'd seen her body enough as he worked with her over the last month.

Images of her stretching and sweating assailed him until he pushed them firmly out of his mind or he'd go find her and fuck her against the trunk of the nearest tree. God, he wanted her bad and he knew she wanted him too. That was the kicker. This artificial barrier she'd created over their age difference was just dumb and she was using it to keep him away.

As he turned the corner he saw her with Bill, head tipped up, body leaning into his as they watched the sky. As if Marc had called her name, she turned toward him. Her gaze caught his for long moments until she let go and returned her attention to the fireworks.

Frustrated, he glanced back toward the blankets where Becky Sue waited with Cassie, Shane, Maggie and Kyle. He smiled when he caught Kyle placing his palms over Maggie's growing baby bump. They were good together.

He froze a moment. Marriage? Liv said she wanted long term. Said she wanted to get married. Okay, so he wasn't too young to have a nice fling with her but he was definitely not interested in marriage. *Yikes.* No, he'd go back to being her friend, sport a few furtive fantasies about bedding her and continue on with his happily unencumbered life. Marriage was for suckers and he was most certainly not a sucker. Yeah, sure.

৪০৪০০৪

Friends my ass, Marc thought as he watched her take another lap in the community pool one Saturday morning a month after that kiss. She was made for the water, swam like a freaking seal and, even in a non-descript one piece swimsuit, she looked hot.

He shouldn't even be there. He didn't need to be. Her Saturday workouts weren't even in his schedule. But he found himself unable to resist being near her when he could be.

"Hey there!" she called out as she pulled herself out of the water and grabbed a nearby towel. "Whatcha doing here?"

He stared at her a moment, watching the water beaded like diamonds on her thick lashes, her dark hair slicked back against her head.

"I played racquetball with Kyle earlier. We just finished and I saw you and thought I'd come say hello." He looked at her upper body and nodded. "You're really coming along, Liv. Your shoulders look fantastic."

She blushed and he cursed his ridiculously friendly cock for bounding to attention.

"Thank you. Two months of working out will do that, I suppose. At first I thought it'd be hard to work it into my schedule, but really, it's not that bad and I'm used to it now. Plus, I like the way I feel."

He liked *her.* Damn it. This friends stuff wasn't cutting it. He'd gone out with every woman he could but none of them could get his mind off Liv.

"What are you up to just now? I haven't had any lunch. You hungry?" He sent her his best, *just friends* smile as he lied through his teeth.

"I'm actually meeting Cassie and Maggie for lunch in about forty-five minutes. Sorry. I'd invite you but we're going to be talking about babies and then sex and stuff you aren't privileged to hear." She grinned and his gut tightened.

"Fine, fine. Keep me out of all the fun. See if I care." He heaved a theatrical sigh. "Looks like I'll try and catch up to Kyle and Shane as they'll be free. I'll see you Monday then. Have a good weekend."

She waved as she headed toward the locker area and he watched the sway of that delectable ass before making up his mind and heading out to catch up to Kyle.

"Kyle!" Marc shouted as he jogged toward his brother.

Kyle tossed his bag into the back seat and turned. "What's up?"

"I need your help." He briefly filled his brother in.

"Meet me at my house in an hour. I'll call Shane and have him bring some take out."

Relieved, Marc nodded and headed home to change.

ಐಷಿ೦೫

Liv looked at herself in her rearview mirror when she pulled up to the restaurant. At least the strain didn't show. Every time she saw Marc she wanted to kiss him. But he was off the menu. And he hadn't shown anything but a friendly regard for her since that night anyway. And why not? She was hot, damn it!

Oh she cracked herself up. Yeah, right. It wasn't funny that she could not shake this insane jones for Marc Chase.

The marriage comment freaked him out. And good. It wouldn't be right for her to engage in a dalliance with him when she knew it wouldn't go anywhere. *No*, she was done with that. It was time to look past tomorrow morning. It was time she did something for herself and chose a man who wanted to share his tomorrows with her, not just his night and a few condoms.

Man, self respect blew sometimes.

Chapter Four

Marc let himself into Kyle and Maggie's place and followed the sound of his brothers to the kitchen where they were busily opening up boxes of food.

"Hey there. Grab a beer, we'll get to work in a minute," Kyle called out. Marc cracked a cold one open and sat down at the table in the breakfast nook.

"Didn't expect it to be a full house."

Matt rolled his eyes. "We're brothers. Between the four of us, we've handled a whole lot of women. Kyle tells me this is a woman issue. Let's hear it. Between all of us, we can solve just about anything."

Shane chuckled and bit into a spring roll. "Spill."

Kyle nodded.

"It's Olivia." He looked to Matt nervously, now understanding why Kyle invited him. It would be best to do this all openly so Matt wouldn't be upset.

"What about her?" Matt watched him suspiciously.

"I have a thing for her something fierce. It's not just lust, although I have that in spades. Oh man do I have that." Marc shook his head. "It's more. I kissed her at the Founder's Day Picnic. It was," he licked his lips, "specfuckingtacular. I've never, ever, felt that way kissing a woman. And I haven't been able to forget it. I want to be with her but she doesn't take me seriously."

"What did she say?" Shane asked.

"First she said she was too old for me. Dumbest thing I ever heard. Has the woman never looked in a mirror? She's amazing. I told her it was only six years. And then she said she wasn't looking for one night or one week." He heaved a sigh. "I know. She's right to distrust me on that score. She says she's not going out with men who only want something temporary anymore. She says we can only be friends." He rolled his eyes at that.

"And clearly you don't want that. But what do you want because, Marc, she's telling you what she does. She doesn't want to be temporary. You're a temporary kind of guy." Kyle watched his brother carefully.

Marc scrubbed his hands over his face. "I know. I know what I am. What I *was*. And she's right to turn me down based on what she's seen. It's not like I've made a secret of it. But you all know." He looked at Matt and laughed before turning back to Kyle. "Well, you and Shane know what it is when you want to cast that aside for something lasting."

"You saying you're in love with Liv?" Matt asked, incredulous. "You, Mister Different-woman-on-his-arm-every-night?"

"I'm not in love with Olivia, no. I don't know her well enough. Not like that. But I do know I want more than a week or two with her. I want to explore something long term. For real. I've gotten to know her as a person, not as my brother's girlfriend and then ex. I'd like to get to know her as a woman now. But I don't know how to get her to trust me enough to let me in."

"And that's where we come in," Kyle said, clinking his beer against Shane's. "Liv needs a good old-fashioned wooing."

Shane chuckled. "You ready to woo? It's like training for a marathon, Marc. She doesn't trust you and that's based on what she's seen for years. You're going to have to forego other women. Can you do that?"

"Yes. I've tried to date Liv out of my head but it hasn't worked. I'm not interested in anyone else. She takes up my mind every minute of the damned day."

"Olivia is a good woman. Beautiful, giving. Can you take care of that? Work to not hurt her?" Matt asked.

"I can. I swear to you all that I would not be pursuing this if I thought it was just some temporary thing. I don't want to hurt her. I know she deserves more than that. I want to give her more than that."

Matt sighed and held up his beer. "Well then, let's work on the woo, shall we? Four Chase boys all united? She doesn't stand a chance."

⍟⍟⍟

Monday evening, Liv walked into Marc's Body By Design and smiled when she saw him there. He sat on his haunches next to one of the machines, talking to Shane.

Boy did they both look fine. Shane was huge. Muscled, hard and now sweaty. She did like that Shane's workout coincided with hers. She loved Cassie to pieces and would never dream of taking on a pain in the ass man like Shane Chase. But he sure was nice to look at.

Then again Marc—with his muscled thighs straining against his shorts and the hard muscles of his back and shoulders visible through the neck of the T-shirt he wore—was a hundred times hotter. He carried his strength easily, gracefully.

She had to gulp and hurry past them to drop her stuff off in a locker before she leapt on him and licked his neck. Why oh why did the sight of a bead of sweat rolling down to the hollow of his throat make her itchy to lick him? Wasn't that sick? That was it. She was sick and perverted. Sweat making her hot, good gracious she needed sex.

When she came out, Shane was leaving. He waved to her, said he was on his way home to shower with Cassie and, leaving her blushing, walked out the door.

Chuckling, Marc accompanied her to the mat where she sat and began to stretch.

"How are you tonight?"

"Good. Stressful day. Budget time. The mayor is cranky and taking it out on everyone. I wanted to bop him on the head with my stapler today."

He took her arms and pulled, letting her stretch her thighs and back. Standing, he reached down, giving her a hand up.

They headed to the free weights where she began her first rep of thirty. "You need me to kick his ass? John always has been kinda punky."

Liv laughed. "Thank you for that very chivalrous offer, Marc, but I think I scared him back in line. He's not a bad guy, he's just a control freak and you can't control everything at this time of year."

He reached out to correct her arm. "This way. You're going to hurt yourself if you do it like that. You sure look pretty tonight."

She looked at him askance. "Uh, yeah. Straining muscles and T-shirts with exercise shorts always make a girl look pretty. You need a loan or something?"

He barked a surprised laugh. "I'm good. Business is doing well as it happens and you do look pretty. I like the new thing you're doing with your hair. It was sort of sleek and straight last month but I like this tousled, curly thing you're doing."

Liv stilled mentally. It wasn't so much that he was flirting. She could handle flirting. He was...earnest. Sincere. It was off-putting because while she could blow off flirting, sincere compliments and a keen interest in her and her perspective from him felt intimate and had the added effect of making her all tingly. Lawd. She was such a loser.

"Uh, thanks." *Uh thanks?* Could she be any less coherent? "So, how's your mom?"

"She's good. Says you should come to dinner soon. She and I were talking about you yesterday and we both agreed you don't come around near enough."

Liv put the barbells back and moved to the next station to work her legs. "What's your game, Marc?" She grunted as she pushed the weights the first time. Lovely. Grunting.

"No game. Why do you ask? That's a very half-assed rep, Olivia. Work it, don't puss out."

"Puss out? I most certainly do not *puss out*. I'm tired."

"You're pussing out. Now work it. Your ass will thank you. And I will thank you because you have a very nice ass. You should come with me to open mic night at Lindy's tomorrow. You like live music, don't you?"

She stopped outright. How did he expect her to concentrate when he stood there all hard and yummy, acting sincere and then asking her on a date?

"We went through this already, Marc Chase." Gawd, even she didn't believe the conviction in her voice.

"Stop slacking, Livvy. Move those legs or I'm gonna make you run an extra mile on Wednesday morning."

She snorted. He was gonna make her? "I'll have you know I now run Monday, Wednesday and Friday. I run lots of extra miles." She gritted her teeth and pushed out the last four reps, sweat beading on her temples.

"Good for you."

She heard him arranging the weights as she settled in, grabbed the bar above her head and pulled, working her biceps and shoulders.

He leaned over, his mouth just a whisper from her ear as he adjusted her hands on the bar. "You smell good, too. No chemicals, all woman. I like that."

"I can't concentrate when you do that." Her voice came out breathy and she felt faint.

"What?" He straightened and indicated with a nod that she continue. "Talking about how good you smell messes with your concentration?"

"You know damned well it does. What are you up to, Marc?"

"Finish up." The bastard sauntered away and made some notes, so she ignored him and completed that set. He left her alone for the next two machines but came back into her space when she did her lunges.

"Good. I like the way you're holding your back. Nice work."

She was suspicious, yes, but his praise warmed her despite that.

When she was done, she hurried into the back to change and get going. She'd shower at home and she wanted to get out of there before the giggly client came in. One of the Scott girls if she wasn't mistaken. Couldn't be over twenty-three and the mere sight of her made Liv want to scream and snatch her bald for fawning all over Marc.

When she came out he was waiting. Alone. The lights were turned off but for the very front spots and he had a messenger bag slung across his shoulders.

"Ready?"

"For what? Where's the bottle blonde who giggles incessantly?"

Marc reddened and choked back a smile. "Sarah? She has evening classes this quarter at the community college so she comes in during the afternoons now. Shall I tell her you were asking after her?"

"Yeah sure, smartass. Well, I'll see you Wednesday then."

"Wait. I'm all done for the evening. Let me walk with you. It's a nice night."

Liv narrowed her eyes. "You live in the opposite direction."

"I know. I want to walk with you. Is that a crime?"

"I'm not kissing you or inviting you in." God knew if she invited him in, she'd be naked with him inside her within three minutes.

"Well, we can work up to that. It's a fine evening and I like your company. Come on. I'll be a total gentleman."

She sighed. "Fine. On the way you can tell me your game, Marc."

He locked up behind himself and chuckled as he joined her. "Sugar, I am not playing a game. This is serious. I mean to woo you, so shut up and let me do it."

A burst of pleasure broke over her at his statement even when she knew she should be stern. "You're going to woo me?"

"With every ounce of effort I possess. You don't stand a chance, Liv. You could just give in now and save me the work but I doubt you will. Enjoy it. I know I am."

"What do you think you're going to get out of this? I've said I'm looking for something long term. You're not a long term guy."

He took her hand and looked deep into her eyes. "I didn't use to be, no. But I find myself thinking in terms of what it would be like to take you camping over the summer. Do you ski? I know of some excellent places to get in good winter skiing. I love to take trips and travel around." He paused when they reached the walk in front of her little house. "Look, Liv, I know you don't have any reason to believe me right now. We both know my history. I can't wish it away or pretend it didn't happen. So I'm going to show you I've turned over a new leaf. Prepare to have the hell wooed out of you."

Bringing the hand he'd been holding to his mouth, he brushed his lips over her knuckles and her nipples hardened. She only barely held back a whimper.

"Marc, you're wasting your time," she whispered. "Don't do this to me. Please. You and I both know you don't do women for longer than what, a week or two? You're only interested in me because it's a novelty for you to be turned down."

"I'm genuine here, Liv. I thought so at first too. The novelty thing I mean. But I know different and so will you." He took a step backwards. "I'll see you Wednesday morning then. Have a good night."

She tried to speak but he shook his head and she sighed, moving up the walk to her front door. "See you Wednesday. Thanks for walking me home," she called out.

"My pleasure." He waved and sauntered back the way they'd come.

Man, if he wasn't kidding she was in big trouble. Fear crouched low for a moment and was gone.

ಖುಖುCಇ

He wasn't kidding. Damned Marc Chase! She frowned as she looked at the pretty bouquet of French lavender sitting on her desk. His note said that he hoped the scent would help bring her calm in a stressful time at work. Two days before it had been a raisin muffin from The Honey Bear. A healthy treat. Thoughtful and she loved raisins too.

He'd jogged up to her house with it fresh, still warm from the oven.

Heaving a sigh, she sat down and tried to do her work but the scent of lavender wafted around her as she did.

"Pretty flowers. New admirer?" Maggie grinned at her. "Aren't you done yet? You can tell me who sent these on the way to get Cassie."

"I...uh." She sighed. Liv hadn't told Maggie, or anyone else for that matter, about Marc's declaration of wooage just yet. She didn't know what to think much less how to describe it. She shook her head as she shut her computer down and turned to get out of her chair.

"I'm going to run home first, take these there. I don't want them here over the weekend where they'll just die." Liv grabbed the flowers. "I'll meet you at The Pumphouse."

They walked out together and Maggie headed one way while Liv headed home. Once there, she put the lavender on her kitchen table and headed to her room to change her clothes and touch up her makeup.

She looked in the mirror as she freshened her lipstick. Not bad for a woman who'd be thirty-five in six weeks. She probably should have stayed out of the sun more. Wore sunscreen. God, how was she supposed to know it was bad to cook herself every summer until she got a good base tan? Everyone knew you had to get a few good burns before your skin got nice and dark. She sighed. And now it caused cancer.

"Stop it now before you turn into one of those crazy cat ladies, Olivia Jean," she admonished herself in the mirror.

At The Pumphouse, Cassie and Maggie were already waiting. It was a bit lonelier without Dee there but Dee would be spending less and less time in Petal now that she and Arthur had moved to Atlanta and their house had just sold.

"Scooch over, hot stuff," Liv said to Cassie. She tried not to look toward the back where the pool tables were. If Marc was there she'd end up staring at him all night.

"So, flowers huh? Who?" Cassie poured Liv a beer and pushed the glass toward her.

"Did y'all order the chili cheese fries yet? I ran an extra mile this morning and I'm starving." Liv busied herself looking through her purse.

"Hoo boy! This is good. You won't even look me in the eye. It's Roger Petrie isn't it? You've decided you can overcome his, erm, intense love of his animals." Maggie laughed.

Roger Petrie was one of the oddest citizens in town. Well known for his predilection for keeping his animals in bed with him.

Liv stopped rustling around and looked up at her friends. Cassie snickered and Liv just shook her head. "You're totally insane. No. That's not it. You're *jealous*. Ha! Roger is all mine, baby. Between me and his goat, there's no room left in his bed."

Maggie tossed her head back and laughed until her eyes teared up.

"If you must know, it's Marc."

Maggie stopped laughing and looked over at Liv, mouth open in shock. "Marc Chase sent you flowers? Why?"

"He tells me he's wooing me."

"Oh the woo." Cassie blew out a breath. "They're awfully good at the woo, those boys."

"No shit. Kyle wooed my panties right off. Wooed ice cream in my belly button at three in the morning." Maggie sighed. "Damn good woo. I'm betting they got it from Edward. It's always the quiet ones. But why is he wooing you?"

"What? You don't think I'm worthy of woo?"

"Say that five times fast." Cassie laughed. "No, cupcake. I think Maggie is asking why a man with a revolving door in his bedroom is wooing a woman who's declared she's looking for more than a few nights' entertainment. Has something happened?"

"Yeah. What she said. Of course you're worthy of woo. Dumbass."

"You're very cranky now that you're knocked up." Liv couldn't help but turn, and damn if her eyes didn't move straight to Marc's ass. "Boy howdy the man has an ass on him."

The other two women craned their necks to look. "Oh yeah. The nicest of the bunch ass-wise, I'd wager. Back to you telling us what's going on," Cassie said.

Reluctantly, Liv turned back to her friends and told them the whole story. Including the night of the Founder's Day picnic up until the flowers he'd had delivered that morning.

"Wow. Well, if I may direct you to a statement you made to me in this very booth nearly two years ago now. You said, *when a man like that falls, he falls hard and all the way. There's no middle ground for a guy like Shane.* Now, I think you can turn that around and say the same of Marc. If he says he wants more, I believe him. He may be a randy little dude, but he's a good-hearted, honest man. And he wouldn't pursue you if he didn't think he could give you what you want." Cassie grabbed a fry and popped it in her mouth.

"He's not offering marriage. He's wooing me. God help me, that's enough."

Maggie waved that away. "None of these men are going to offer you marriage from date one. Well, maybe Roger if you buy him some goat chow. But what if? What if this could develop into something real?"

"Goat chow, you're a laugh riot. And I don't know. I've had my heart trampled on and I don't want to go back there again. I'm afraid."

Cassie put her arm around Liv's shoulders. "Ah cupcake, I know that feeling. But you say you want to find something real. Someone real. You'll never know if you don't let it happen. He won't cheat on you. He's too honorable for that. And he's, well I've seen him in his swim trunks out on my dock swimming in the lake and when I say little dude, I'm just being affectionate. I don't think it's an accurate way to describe his body at all."

"Don't I know it? Good gracious, when we're running and he takes off his shirt to wipe his face? Oh, I want to lick him. But he's so young. I feel like a cradle robber."

"Will you quit it with that already? Not quite six years' difference. You're hot, he's hot for you. What's the issue? He's certainly old enough to knowingly consent. And here's the thing, go out with him and see. If it's not a love match, keep with your plan but you have to date to find Mister Right anyway, don't you?" Maggie sipped her soda and smiled.

༺ఴఴ༻

Marc saw her come in and nearly ripped the felt with his cue. She was all leggy grace and energy and he loved the shiny lipstick she had on. Reminded him of raspberries.

"Holy moley she looks good enough to eat," he murmured.

Matt chuckled and took his turn. "How goes the woo?"

"She got all stuttery when I brought her the muffin on Wednesday morning and I had lavender sent to her office today. She said it was stressful because it was budget time. Lavender is good for calming and relaxing. I thought it might help."

"Oh that's good. Damn, you're diabolical, little brother." Kyle looked over at the three women gathered in their usual booth. "She sure is pretty."

"She's beautiful. I love her laugh. And she's cocky, I like that. Called Sarah Scott a giggly bottle blonde."

Matt laughed. "Well she's spot on there. Sarah still trying to get you in her bed, Marc?"

"She's too damned young. She might be twenty-two but mentally she's about sixteen. I don't need that kind of trouble. Never have. No, I prefer trouble with inky black hair and brown cat's eyes."

"You know, if you really want to increase your chances of making this work, you should enlist Momma's help." Shane's gaze drifted to his wife's and Marc felt that tug between them.

"That's true. Neither of these two knuckleheads could have landed such fabulous women without Momma's interference," Matt said.

"Well, certainly not Shane but I landed Maggie myself," Kyle mumbled but Marc ignored him.

"Two steps ahead of you. I just happened to mention to Momma that it had been some time since Liv had been to Sunday dinner. Course Momma gave me grief for bringing it up on a Friday afternoon but agreed with me and said she'd invite her for this Sunday. Do not, however, tell Momma I'm interested in Liv. I want to do this my own way and Momma will get up in my business."

"I don't know how you could talk about her that way, Marc. Momma just likes to help." Matt snickered.

"You wait, Matt Chase. It'll be your turn one of these days. And I'm gonna laugh and laugh." Marc grunted once he'd made his shot.

After a few games, it was time to get going. Kyle and Shane wanted to get home with their wives and Matt had a date to meet across town.

"Liv, can I drop you home?" Marc asked as he caught up with her outside The Pumphouse.

Liv turned and smiled at him and he felt it to his toes. Damn.

"Marc, thank you for the lavender. It was very thoughtful. I walked here. Hope that'll get me some extra credit with my personal trainer. He's such a hard ass." She winked. "Anyway, I was just going to walk home. It's not far and the night is pretty warm. Thanks anyway."

"I'll walk with you then." He caught up to her and easily kept pace as they strolled down Main.

"Your mother called me a few minutes ago. I can't believe she has my cell phone number." Liv laughed.

"Momma's got everyone's number. You'd do well to just accept it. So what'd she want?"

"She invited me to dinner Sunday. Well, no. Invited means I had the option to refuse, I suppose. This was an order, only said in that pretty, pushy way she's got. Butter wouldn't melt in her mouth but it was still an order. Plus she added a twist of guilt. You know, *it's been so long since you've had dinner here. I'm beginning to think you don't like us anymore.*"

Marc burst out laughing. "I see Polly Chase isn't the only one who's got everyone's number. But you said you'd go didn't you?"

"You know I did. Is she in on your plan to woo?"

He put a hand over his chest in mock dismay. "Olivia Davis! I do not need my mother to help me woo a woman. I'm walking you home on a Friday evening. I've been watching you all night long. I don't need her help, thank you very much. My family likes you, Liv. Including my mother. But I'm not going to complain that you're coming to dinner on Sunday. I like looking at you."

They stopped at her front walkway. "Marc, I don't know what to say when you're like this."

"What do you mean? And you should invite me in. Be polite."

She sighed. "If I invite you in, I'll let you kiss me again and then... Well, anyway. It's a bad idea. I mean, when you're genuine I don't know how to respond. You should just flirt with me and go out with giggle girl. I'm not for you."

Marc took her hand and kissed it briefly. "Olivia, that's pretty hurtful. I'm always genuine. Even when I flirt. I'm not shallow and it's not fair of you to say that."

She shook her head. "No, that's not what I meant. I'm sorry. I'm not saying you're shallow. It's just that when you're flirtatious, you're being lighthearted, silly. I can deal with that. Fling it back your way. But when you're..." She pulled her hand away and shoved a curl behind her ear. "I don't know how to say it. I just know how it makes me feel."

Stepping closer to her, he took her hand again. "And how is that?"

"Off balance. Confused." Her voice was no more than a whisper.

"And you don't like not being in control, do you, sugar?" He cocked his head. He should feel bad for her but he had her on the ropes. She was going down and he wasn't going to stop until she had no defenses left. "As for you not being for me? You know that's a lie. Both of us do. You're for me, Olivia Davis. All long legs and big brown cat eyes. Sex and sin and all sorts of mischief on your face. I like that."

"Oh man. Stop it. This isn't fair."

"Nope. Not fair at all." Quickly, before she could realize his intention, he leaned down and brushed his lips over hers. Just a feather light touch. His body zinged with her taste.

Blinking quickly, those sexy cat eyes looked up into his, surprise and a hint of arousal in them. "I have to go in."

"Go on then. I'll watch you until you're safely inside. I take it you're not inviting me so I'll wait. Bide my time."

He took in the way she had to swallow hard and then watched as she gathered her wits about her and took a step back, away from the heat they'd generated. Damn, when they made love the first time it was going to scorch the paint off the walls.

She quickly headed up her walk and rummaged through her bag for her keys. As she unlocked her door she looked back over her shoulder, not speaking for long moments. Finally she said, "Night, Marc. I'll see you Sunday."

He waved and loped back down the sidewalk, grin on his face.

Chapter Five

Liv knew what a mistake accepting the dinner invitation was when she stepped into the foyer of the Chase's home. Marc greeted her, kissing her cheek. But not really her cheek, more like the outermost edge of her mouth.

He smelled good. Different than when they worked out. Marc smelled like warm, sexy man with a bit of cologne. Not too much, but just enough to tickle her senses. And she still wanted to lick him.

"Come on through. Everyone's just hanging out in the living room."

As they'd done when she was with Matt. But for the first time since they'd broken up, she didn't feel that loss when she entered the room where the family had gathered. When she saw Matt sitting there, feet up on the coffee table, she didn't flash to the times they were together. Because Marc took up her thoughts. The way his body was wide at the shoulders but tapered at his waist. The curve of those buns. Yum.

"Hiya, Livvy. Glad you could make it." Edward smiled at her from his recliner.

She smiled back. It was hard not to. Edward Chase was just that kind of man. He smiled and you wanted to smile back as you basked in the warmth of his attention.

Polly moved to give her a quick hug and kiss and Liv settled on one of the couches next to Maggie.

"How's it goin', momma?" Liv touched her friend's belly.

"So much movement now. He, or she is dancing around in there. Going to the doctor next week for another ultrasound. Since they couldn't see the gender last time they're giving me another look. I'm really excited. You're still coming, right?"

"Dude, like I'd miss it? Has Kyle changed his mind yet about wanting to know?"

Maggie shook her head. "No. He'll leave the room when they tell me. And you're sworn to silence around him."

"I want it to be a surprise. It'll be cool, don't you think?" Kyle leaned over Maggie.

"I'm not getting into this one. Uh uh." Liv put her hands up.

"Smart girl. Let's all go in to eat," Polly called out from the doorway.

The Kyle-Maggie baby gender discussion continued at one end of the table while Liv tried not to stare at Marc.

"It sure is nice to have you back at our table, Olivia," Polly passed a platter of her famous smothered pork chops her way.

"It's nice to be here." Liv concentrated on only taking one chop. They smelled so good her mouth watered. "Especially on pork chop night."

Marc laughed. "She is a mighty fine cook."

Marc liked seeing her back at their table too. She fit there with them. As Maggie's best friend and one of Cassie's closest friends, the connections were there. And his mother clearly adored her, which was half the battle. Woe be to any woman one of them wanted if Polly didn't approve.

There was an element of comfort there, but also of *knowing*. She belonged at that table. At his side. Man, he had it bad and he wanted her to have it bad too.

At the end of the evening, Liv helped clear the table while the guys did the clean up. Marc watched her, so animated and vivacious. Sharp-witted, clever and bright.

"Son, you're besotted," Edward murmured as he approached Marc. "Don't think I've noticed you look at Olivia that way before. She know?"

Marc sighed. "She does. Well she knows I'm interested but she doesn't think I'm serious. She thinks I'm just out for a one night stand."

Edward looked him up and down. "Ah, it's uncomfortable when your past comes to bite you on the butt, isn't it, son? One of these days I may just tell you a story about me and your momma. Suffice it to say, Chase men like to run and hunt but once we find our woman, that's it. There's no one else for us. You saying Olivia is the one?"

"Dad, I don't know. All I know is that I've never felt this way about anyone before. I want more than a few weeks. I like seeing her here. Like feeling she's one of us."

"How does your brother feel? I expect you'd have discussed this with him?"

Marc nodded as he looked to Matt, who was joking and flirting with Cassie. "I did. He was worried I'd hurt her but he says he's behind me and this woo plan one hundred percent. I wouldn't want him to feel bad. He knows she wasn't the one for him. And it's been two years now that they've been broken up."

"Okay then. Well, boy, you let me know if I can help in any way. I do like Olivia quite a bit. She's a good woman. The kind of woman who'll be a true partner and won't run when things get rough. But you'll have to catch her first because she's gonna run from you 'til you catch her."

Marc laughed and the woman in question turned to face him, a question in those eyes of hers. He winked and she shook her head, turning back to his mother.

Later, he insisted on walking her to her car. "Good night, Olivia. I'll see you tomorrow." His fingers itched to touch her, mouth watered to taste her.

"Night, Marc."

"Don't suppose you'd let me kiss you just now?" He took a step closer so their bodies were just an inch apart.

"I..." She gulped and nodded. Triumph roared through him and he leaned toward her.

"Liv! You forgot your leftovers!" Polly called as she came out the front door.

Liv jumped and opened her door quickly, tossing her purse inside. "Oh, thank you, Mrs. Chase. You didn't need to do that."

Marc wanted to scream in frustration as he found himself jogging up to grab the bag from his mother. "I've got it, Momma."

"Of course I didn't need to. I wanted to. Now go on, drive safe, honey and I'll see you soon. You need to come back to dinner again. Don't make me hunt you down." Polly waved and stayed put on the porch as Marc handed the leftovers to Liv, wanting to groan as she bent to load them into her passenger seat. Her ass swayed a bit with the movement.

"Okay then. Good night." Liv waved at Polly and sent Marc a rueful smile. "See you tomorrow."

"Yeah. I'm collecting on that kiss. Very soon." He closed the door and rapped the top of her tiny little sports car as she drove off.

ಸಿಬ್ಬಿಂ

Liv didn't know whether to be frustrated or relieved that Polly had interrupted the two of them the evening before.

She smiled as she thought about the slim book of poetry she'd found on her desk when she returned from lunch. Maya Angelou's, *Phenomenal Woman* and the little card said, *takes one to know one.* Lawd. Poetry.

But right then her thighs burned through the hell on earth that was Stairmaster time. While she tried to ignore the presence of other people, two of them female who flirted outrageously with Marc. And he returned that attention.

It was his nature she knew. But it still made her sad. She wanted to believe she was different and truth be told, he'd made her feel different too. But the other women. Man, she didn't know if she could deal with it. Maggie had to, Liv knew that first hand. The women in town responded to all the Chase brothers. It was impossible not to, they were loveable rascals and damned good-looking. Kyle had taken Maggie's feelings to heart and made a concerted effort to never be more than generically friendly to other women. Women fell all over themselves for Shane but he didn't spare a second glance at anyone other than his wife.

But Marc wasn't hers. No. They hadn't even dated so her being jealous over flirting was just dumb. And anyway, if she really wanted Marc Chase, she could have him and these little gym bunnies didn't stand a chance. Liv might be older than they were but she had a lot more experience under her belt, not to mention more intelligence and personality too.

Sniffing with her own self-righteous superiority, she rejoiced when her time was up and she was free of the wretched torture device from hell.

"Good job, Liv. Your stamina has really increased." Marc came over and noted her progress.

"Yes, well. I'm through for the night. I'll see you Wednesday. Oh and thank you for the book. I love that poem."

He insisted she cool down and stretch before going to change. "I'm glad. I heard her read it on Oprah or something a few years ago. I always thought it was a great poem and I'm fortunate to have many wonderful women in my life. But it seemed perfect for you."

The hand he'd been using to make sure she extended her back properly continued to rest there as she finished up.

"I'm sorry we got interrupted last night," he murmured. "I have two more clients to see tonight or I'd walk you home."

She smiled. "Do your work. I'll see you Wednesday."

"What? No comment on being interrupted?" He pouted and it was pretty devastating.

"My goodness. I bet that face got you out of a lot of trouble over your life."

He chuckled. "Some. Come on, Liv. I'm fishing here. Give a guy a break."

She softened. He was very bad for her self control. "Okay. I'm sorry we got interrupted too. But it's probably for the best."

"It's not for the best, Olivia. In any case, it was only a temporary reprieve. I'm coming for you." He grinned.

"Oh man. Go on, your little booster club is waiting. I'll see you Wednesday." She turned and put a little extra sway in her walk. She knew she was teasing but she wanted him to think of her instead of those two bimbettes.

All the way home she thought of how his eyes darkened just a bit every time he made a move. They didn't change when he flirted. But when he was down to serious business, they darkened from a blue-green to a deep mossy color.

She could not allow this silly flirtation to derail her plans. She needed to find Mister Right and keep her eyes on the prize. It was libido versus brain, she had to keep her brain in charge.

೮೦ജ಄೮෫

"So, now that we know you're having a boy, I can tell you I went on a date last night." Liv sipped her tea and looked at Cassie and Maggie. They'd had the ultrasound appointment and it had been pretty clear right away that the bundle of Chase in Maggie's belly came with a crank handle.

"Kyle will be begging to know in a week." Cassie laughed and then turned to Liv. "Date with who?"

"Rancher Bill. I also signed up with one of those computer dating places. Of course I got like six hundred emails this morning. Man. You should see some of the stuff they sent me. I wanted to hose off with Lysol afterward."

"Well that's what? Date number three with Bill? How'd it go? Any action yet?" Maggie stole a fry from Cassie's plate. "It totally sucks that you're healthy girl all the sudden, Liv. Less fries to steal. You do, however, look even better than you did before and that was pretty smokin' hot to start with. Thank goodness I'm spoken for or I'd be jealous."

Liv fluttered her lashes. "Why thank you. Marc has really worked me hard. Heh, okay that sounds dirty. Some action with Bill. He's a very good kisser. There was, erm, third base type stuff going on."

"Third base, huh? And how are his hands?" Cassie asked without a blush.

"Lawd you women are deviants. Sheesh." Liv winked. "He's fine. I mean, he's got nice sized equipment. He seemed kind of shy about it." Liv shrugged. "I'm sure when we do sleep together it'll be nice."

"Nice? Since when did you settle for nice? And what about Marc working you hard? What's going on with that?" Maggie demanded.

"What about it? Look, I want to be married, damn it. I want forever. A house. Kids. Pancakes every Sunday. You have that, Maggie and your whole life changed. You're having a child with the man you love. I want that too. I've wasted nearly thirty-five years on men who don't fucking care about me enough to make a baby with me. It's easy for you to sit there and judge, damn it. You have forever." She looked to Cassie. "And you too. Yes, Marc is still wooing and all that but I have a plan. And yes, it's sexy and flattering and he and I have major chemistry. I can't deny it any more than I can stop looking because Marc Chase may be interested in fucking me. Letting myself be distracted by the shiny of hot men like Marc instead of focusing on men who are ready to offer me forever like Bill."

The rigidity in Maggie's spine eased and she sighed. "It's more than that. Liv, I've seen the way he watches you. If all he wanted was to fuck, he'd have moved on by now because you haven't given him any. He hasn't dated in months. I asked Kyle. Don't settle for heaven's sake. You don't have to choose Marc if that's not what you want but if Rancher Bill doesn't rev your motor, there are other men out there. Marriage is forever. If the sex is mundane, it's forever mundane. You're an awfully sexual woman to just accept mediocre." Maggie stared at her, exasperated.

"I've gone that route. Chosen the hot guy with the great chemistry in bed. And it got me nothing but heartache. Maybe I need someone calm. Something calm."

"Fuck that. You don't need something calm. You're lively and you need a man who appreciates that. A laid back man? Sure, given your level of activity and your personality, that might be a good idea. But Liv, you can have great sex and love. Maggie and I do. Dee and Penny do. Not with each other, *that* sounded dirty." Cassie winked at Maggie, who laughed. "You don't have to settle on forever. I understand you want to be married. I support your plan and I love you. But don't just roll over and give up."

"And has it ever occurred to you, Liv, that you wimp out when it comes to the men you choose? I mean, you choose the Rancher Bills of the world over the guys who could be the real thing for some reason? Protecting yourself or something?" Maggie sighed.

"And has it ever occurred to you that not everyone has a wham-pow connection like you and Kyle? Bill is a nice man. I said his hands were nice. He's a good kisser. He hasn't proposed, it's just been three dates. Yes there are other men out there. I'm not settling. I'm simply asking myself if I've been looking for the wrong thing. And what, choosing a marriage minded man over a man like Marc is me protecting myself? That's just dumb. I'm choosing better than I have before. People live without grand passion and have spouses they admire and respect and live quite happily."

"I see your chin getting all stubborn, Olivia Davis. Stop it. We're your friends. If we don't tell you like it is, who will? All I'm saying is that you can have great sex, great chemistry and forever," Maggie said, one eyebrow rising.

Liv waved it away. "I'm not stubborn. I have to get back to work. I'll see you all Friday if not before."

"Not stubborn my ass," Cassie murmured. "I only know one person more stubborn than you and I'm married to him."

Liv drank the last of her tea and stood. "I am not even in Shane's league, stubborn wise. You however, are right up there, missy." She kissed the top of Maggie's head and blew one to Cassie. "I'll see you all later. I appreciate the honesty. I do."

And she did. They were right, she knew. But it was just three dates with Bill, she'd see him again if he called. It wouldn't kill her to give the man another chance.

ഇൻഈരു

The Pumphouse was packed to the gills, which only agitated Marc more than he already was. He kept looking toward the front and seeing Liv there, laughing with his sisters-in-law.

He also kept seeing various men stop by the table to flirt with her. Oh how he hated that. Everywhere she went she turned heads with that smile. And the bright red, very small top and the white pants she wore that night only highlighted the pale beauty of her skin and the darkness of her hair, which she'd changed again; this time it stood up in a sort of spiky disarray. A bit rock and roll. One of her shoes, a high heeled slide, dangled from her toes as she slowly kicked her foot back and forth under the table.

"You look like a lovesick puppy. I'd be snickering that a woman finally turned the tables on you but I feel too sorry for you. What's the next step in Plan Woo?" Matt clapped him on the shoulder.

"Picnic. I've got the stuff out in my truck. I want to take her out to the lake under the stars. Good heavens, look at Frank Gillchrist. He's making a damned fool out of himself with her. Practically taking up residence in the front of her shirt."

"Go on. Get out of here. You're miserable and you're going to start a fight with someone if you don't just make your move already." Shane took his shot and bumped Marc hip to hip.

"If it brings you any comfort, she's been sneaking looks back here for the last hour." Matt smirked.

"Some. Okay, I'm gone. Wish me luck." Marc put his cue back on the wall and headed toward her booth, single mindedly ignoring the women who put themselves in his path.

She looked up at him with a tentative smile. "Hey there, Marc Chase."

"You and me, picnic under the stars. What do you say?" He held out a hand.

A moment passed and he wanted to kick himself for putting it that way until she grabbed her purse and took his hand. "All right then."

Well, that was pleasant. If only she let him have his way in everything. Maggie looked up at him through her lashes, a smile playing on her lips. Retribution lay just beyond the encouragement. If he damaged Liv, Maggie would kick his ass. And then Cassie would have a go.

Marc smiled at Maggie and blew her a kiss and, as he didn't play favorites with his gorgeous sisters-in-law, he sent one Cassie's way as well. "See y'all later." Placing Liv's hand in the crook of his arm, he escorted her out and to his truck.

"What is it with you boys and these trucks? I mean, if I didn't know better, I'd think you all were overcompensating for other things that weren't so big."

Surprised, Marc snorted a laugh. "How do you know better, Miz Liv? You been peeking into the men's locker room?"

Opening the passenger door for her, he watched appreciatively as she scrambled up into the seat.

"Wouldn't you like to know?" Liv replied with a smug smirk, making him laugh again. Damn he liked her attitude.

He jogged around to the driver's side and got in. As they drove away from the center of town, he snuck a look at her. He'd like to know, hell yes. But he'd show her himself and he hoped like hell it would be soon or his cock would fall off from disuse.

Liv sat in the giant truck, watching the skies darken into evening. She should not be there with this man. A picnic under the stars alone was a very bad idea. Alone with him was a bad idea but when he'd stalked over and got all bossy, it made her weaken inside. Something about it when he took charge made her all gooey.

He'd looked commanding in those snug jeans and the cowboy boots. His brothers didn't wear boots very often but he did and she thought it was sexy. His shirt flowed over the muscles of his upper body like a caress. Not tight, that would have been tacky, but the material definitely showcased his strength.

She didn't like to be bossed around and she hadn't met a man who could ably take charge of her in the bedroom. She managed her life quite well and was happy being an independent woman. That didn't mean a very in charge, dominant man wasn't the most delicious fantasy she had. And an unfulfilled one too.

He pulled down a long road toward the lake and parked. "Those are some pretty shoes so I won't make you walk too far. It's just down the path. I saw this little spot when I came out to row the other day. Shane and Cassie's place is just across the way."

Rowing must be why his upper body looked so damned good. "Well, it's working for you. Maybe I'll give it a try sometime. I've only used the machine but it seems like it'd be fun."

"It is. The water is nice and if you come out early enough, it's quiet and beautiful and the water is smooth as glass. Hang on a sec."

He got out and grabbed the ice chest from the bed of the truck and met her around on her side where, he was pleased to see, she'd waited for him.

Instead of waiting for her to get out, he banded her waist with his arm and pulled her down, sliding her body against his until her toes touched the ground.

"Mmm, you feel good," he murmured, nuzzling the hollow of her throat instead of kissing those lips. He'd wanted to but he'd save it. Savor it. "Come on."

She took his hand and they walked down a path to a grassy slope that led to the shoreline. He spread a blanket down and she kicked off her shoes before sitting.

He joined her, sitting next to her instead of across from her. With a small smile, he unloaded the cooler, placing the food out in front of them.

"Wow. Impressive. Did you make all this?" Liv swept her hand, indicating the array of goodies.

"Hell no. I wish. This is from that new deli that opened up on Elm and Fourth. Roasted vegetables, fresh feta cheese, fruit of all kinds, I got the bread from the bakery, it's some sort of flatbread the guy said. Turkey, olives and oh..." he pulled out a white bakery box, "...cupcakes. Two of them. Butter cream frosting. Because if you can't splurge, life isn't worth living."

"Cupcakes?" Liv sighed dreamily. "I love cupcakes. My goodness, you're perfect. And you got to me just before the food came so I'm starving."

Insanely pleased she'd liked such a small gesture, he grinned as he pulled out some bottled water. "I have wine too if you'd prefer. But when I kiss you, and I will, I want you to be clearheaded."

"Awfully sure of yourself."

He nodded, making himself a sandwich. "I am. Because I want you so much it makes my skin itch. And because I know you want me too."

Her only reply was an intake of breath. He let her hide from answering. For now.

They ate in companionable silence as the night deepened. It was clear and warm and the stars and three quarter moon gave off plenty of light.

She took a sip of water, nervous. What an effect he had on her! No man had ever made her speechless, not even Matt and she had loved him. But this man pushed every button and she wasn't sure why or how. Six months ago he'd been a pretty face she liked to see every few weeks here and there around town and all the sudden she thought of him all the time. Imagined his hands on her, his mouth, wondered about how the heat of his naked skin would feel against hers.

In truth, she should be running back to that truck of his. But her body and libido had firmly refused to comply with her brain and she decided to ride it out, see where things went.

He shifted beside her and her heart kicked in her chest.

"Liv," he said softly and it was as if another woman's hands screwed the top of the water on and placed the bottle aside. She turned to face him and couldn't stop a gasp when she found him so very close.

73

"There you are." He smiled lazily. "You're damned sexy I don't quite know where to start. But I figure the lips are the best first step."

Surely, he moved, closing the last few inches between them. Warm, lush lips covered hers. His hand slid up her back, fingertips teasing her spine and then to her neck and into her hair. He cradled her head, holding her just how he wanted as he deepened the kiss from slow exploration to hungry plunder.

His tongue feathered the seam of her lips and flowed inside when she opened to him. Warm and sinuous, his tongue slid along hers. He wasn't aggressive, but Marc Chase knew what he was about and he kissed her without hesitation. He took what he wanted and gave back in spades.

Liv wasn't shy sexually, she believed very strongly that women had to be in charge of themselves and their pleasure and to demand it if necessary from a partner. But Marc needed no guidance on that score. No wonder the women on his arm always looked happy.

He guided her back to the blanket, his upper body settling against hers. His teeth nipped her bottom lip in short succession, once, twice and then again, his tongue laved the sting away.

She slid her hands under his shirt, exploring the miles of hot, hard muscle there, loving the flex and bunch as she touched him. This was dangerous. Marc wasn't some jovial hunk like Brody had been. This was happening at his pace although he wasn't forcing anything, he was firmly in charge. She normally held the sexual upper hand in the relationship. Damn, perhaps that was why Brody cheated and Matt walked away. Okay, that wasn't something to think on at that moment.

Marc broke the kiss, looking into her face. "You okay? You with me?"

Breathless, she nodded and grabbed his hair, pulling his mouth back to her own.

Marc had to hold his lower body away from hers. If he touched her with his cock she might run away. No, gauging by the way she kissed back, she wouldn't run. But he wanted to fuck her right then, press himself deep into her body and ride her until she begged him to let her come.

And it wasn't time for that just yet. They'd make love, he had no doubt of that. But not out there. He wanted to explore her first. Take his time and make it good. He couldn't do that where they were even if the idea of being caught didn't turn him right on.

Her lips were sweet. Made for him. She was incredibly responsive to his touch, returning his kiss with abandon. And she knew her way around a kiss. This was not some young woman waiting for him to make all the moves. Olivia was not just sexy, she was a woman who enjoyed sex, that much was obvious in her response.

He'd never actually been with a woman he could truly loose all his sexual energies with. The thought that he might be able to with Liv was alluring.

Her hands moved to the waist of his jeans and then to his fly. *Sweet baby Jesus.* He groaned when she grasped his cock, sliding her thumb through the slickness at the head.

"Holy shit. Liv wait." He didn't want her to stop but they couldn't go at it out there.

"Why?" She looked up at him, her face colored by moonlight, a smile tipping one corner of that luscious, kiss-swollen mouth.

"Because when I fuck you, I want you spread out on my bed so I can lick and touch every damned inch of your body. Once you stroke me, I lose all sense of proportion and I don't

Lauren Dane

want the first time you make me come to be out here. I want to come in your mouth, Olivia," he murmured and she shivered and moaned softly.

Gently, he pushed her hands away and sat up, putting the food and trash away. "Come on back to my place."

It wasn't so much a request as an enticing order. Liv's entire body was on fire for him. She needed him inside her so badly her thighs trembled. The truth was, he'd been a surprise. Who'd known he was capable of such control and deep sexuality? He came off as playfully sexual but the comment about coming in her mouth wasn't a line, it was a truth, delivered in a desire-roughened voice, and it set her aflame.

So it wouldn't lead to picket fences but she'd lay good odds it would lead to multiple orgasms and she liked Marc. A lot. What harm could it do at that point to take a little enjoyment in each other until the attraction wore off?

She looked up at him where he stood, cooler in hand. Making up her mind, she grasped his outstretched hand and let him pull her to stand. But he didn't stop there, he grabbed her around her waist and pulled her flush against him.

Lips just a hair's breadth away from hers, he whispered, "I'm going to make you come so many times you're going to pass out by the time I'm finished."

Her heart raced as shivers worked through her body. "Okay."

Chuckling, he let go to grab the blanket and they headed back to his truck where she settled in, looking out over the water while he tucked the cooler into the back and came around to his side.

The quick drive back to town, back to where his apartment sat over a shoe store, was quiet but not uncomfortably so. He pulled into the alley at the rear and parked.

Before she knew it she was in his lap, her body straddling his. She didn't even know why she'd done it but there was certainly no reason to waste her situation.

"That'll do nicely, Liv," Marc said with a wicked grin as his wide palms slid up her legs, stopping at the back of her thighs just below the swell of her ass.

Her lips found his with almost desperate joy. His taste roared through her system, enticing, seductive, making her tremble with need. She swallowed his groan, the sound sliding down her throat as she suckled his tongue. It was probably the lack of sex, but she was pretty sure she'd never wanted a man that desperately before.

She wanted to grind herself over his erection but his hands held her up out of reach. When she whimpered, trying to move down, he chuckled and she found herself on her back on the bench seat.

"That's more like it." Quick hands pulled her pants and the tiny wispy panties off. "So beautiful." His fingertips traced the line of her labia, slick and swollen and she unashamedly widened her thighs to get more of him.

She gasped when he brought those fingertips to his lips, closing his eyes at her taste. "Better than I'd imagined. And I've imagined a lot. Olivia, I'm going to taste you out here where anyone could catch us. You're going to scream when I make you come and then I'm going to fuck you. After that we'll go inside and start again."

Licking her lips at his words, Liv could only manage a nod. Cripes, the man was sex on legs. No one else she'd ever been with could have gotten away with what he'd just said to her. But he more than got away with it, her body, her mind, yearned for more.

"Hands above your head. Hold onto the door." Marc insinuated himself between her thighs, pushing them yet wider and spreading her pussy open before taking a long lick.

Her breath rushed out and pleasure, bright and hot, made her see stars. Her fingers got numb as they dug into the padded door handle. His mouth—tongue, teeth and lips, set about devastating her, driving her toward climax hard and fast.

"Don't rob me of your voice, Olivia," he murmured, stopping for a moment. "I want to hear you. I want to know how I'm making you feel. Stop biting your lip and give me what I want."

All she could do was gasp and then moan when he got back to work. She should be appalled by his behavior but it would be stupid to pretend. And Olivia Davis wasn't stupid.

Instead she complied and let it come as her body primed itself for orgasm. Letting him hear her soft cries and moans as her hips undulated against his mouth.

Satisfaction roared through him as he eagerly took in each sound she made. He'd been surprised when she hopped into his lap and laid some sugar on him after he'd parked but he wasn't one to look away when fate dropped a hot woman in his lap.

He'd push her, see how far she'd let him go, see how much of himself he could be. Embrace the ability to let the full face of his sexuality show and see how hot he could make this beautiful woman spread out on his front seat.

She tasted good, salty-sweet, nearly as good as the moans. Many women hesitated with oral sex, didn't want him to do it, feeling uncomfortable or self conscious. But not this woman. She let herself be held wide open and devoured. He loved that about her.

Loved the way her pussy fluttered around his fingers when he slid them into her, hooking them to stroke over that sweet spot that brought a gasping sob from her lips.

A deep, gut-wrenching groan came from her as she began to come, her back arched, body clenching around his fingers. Gently, he backed away, grabbing a condom from his wallet, freeing his cock, sheathing it and moving to her again.

"Up. I think you need to get back on my lap."

She looked up at him and then down to his cock with a smile. "My, I love a man who's prepared." Scrambling quickly, she held herself above him, reaching around and holding his cock before sliding down, inch by inch until he'd embedded himself fully within the heat of her pussy.

Eye to eye with her, he knew right then. Everything shifted. The noise and chaos in his head, the aching need he felt for her, the confusion that his carefully ordered, commitment free bachelorhood had been discarded and he didn't seem to be bothered—it all fell away. With a sense of clarity he'd never felt before, he saw it. Absolutely without a doubt. He loved Olivia Davis. It should have scared him, freaked him right the fuck out, but it didn't. Instead, a sense of calm settled over him and it was all right. He knew then what Kyle and Shane felt and understood the enormity of the gift he'd been given. Now he had to make sure Liv understood it too but with an inward sigh, he had the feeling it wouldn't be as easy for her.

"Ride me, Liv."

Taking his lips in a kiss, she lifted herself off his cock and slid back down. The pleasure of that heated embrace gathered at the base of his spine as she moved on him, her mouth over his, their tongues sliding together.

He let himself slide toward climax relatively quickly, to take the edge off. Without vanity, he could admit he had a very fast recovery time and he wanted to get her inside where he could stretch out and give every inch of her body the attention it deserved.

Liv bit his bottom lip, slid her tongue through the dimple on his chin, cruised over the line of his jaw as she took him into her body over and over.

She couldn't quite believe she'd let a man go down on her in the front seat of a truck in an alley and now rode him like a pony. All in relative public. And she liked it. Man, she was a deviant because she loved every minute.

Loved it when his fingers found her clit and worked her into another climax and pressed his cock up into her pussy hard and deep as he came. Loved it when he gently sat her beside him and handed her her pants.

"Now that I've taken the edge off, I can dedicate more time to you in the manner you deserve." He tucked her panties into his pocket and his cock back into his pants while she got dressed.

Afterwards, he helped her out of the car and she liked that he kept hold of her hand as they took the stairs up to his place. She'd only been there once before a few years back when Matt had to drop something off.

The first thing she noticed was that it smelled good. She hadn't expected it to. Couldn't say she remembered anything from that last visit but she figured it would smell like most bachelor pads, messy, of unwashed laundry and wet towels.

Marc's place smelled like his cologne and fresh fruit. She saw a set of hanging baskets filled with apples and peaches and knew that's where the scent had come from. His living room windows were large and looked out over the street. It was nicely furnished with bookshelves on the walls and pictures of his family all around.

He kept surprising her and that made her uncomfortable. In the box marked *unavailable bachelor for life*, he was non-threatening because it wouldn't pay to develop feelings for him.

But in the box labeled guy way deeper than she'd thought who loved his family? That guy was dangerous to her well being.

"Now." He flipped the lights off before lighting candles set all around the living room. "I'll be right back." He disappeared down the hall, returning after a few moments. "You look gorgeous with candlelight on your skin. I figured you would. Then again, I've yet to see you in a situation where you didn't look gorgeous."

His hands went to the tie at the right shoulder of her shirt and undid it, letting it fall forward. Her nipples, already hard at his presence, hardened even more at the cool air and the look on his face.

"Okay, let's go down the hall before I take you here on the floor of my living room. I've already had you in a truck, I need to mind my manners now."

She laughed and let him drag her down his hallway to his bedroom. A king sized bed dominated the space.

"I've been dreaming of this," he murmured, pulling his shirt up and over his head. Her heart raced at the sight of him, tawny in the candlelight.

"God you're beautiful."

He stopped and cocked his head, smiling. "Thank you, sugar. I've got nothing on you."

Her blouse lay around her waist and she removed it, laying it on the arm of a chair.

"Nothing on me." She snorted. "Puhleeze. Look at yourself in that mirror there. You're gorgeous. Hard and fit and muscular. I know you know you're handsome, women fall over you all the time and you catch quite a few too."

Chuckling, he unzipped her pants and shoved them down, letting her lean on him as she stepped out of them and her shoes.

"Good gracious." He stalked around her, taking in every inch of her body. A body he'd helped her shape and strengthen. She'd never been ashamed of her nudity but she certainly felt a lot better about her overall tone and shape now that he'd kicked her ass for two and a half months.

"Now you. I want to see all of you."

He stopped in front of her and slowly undid the buttons at the front of his jeans. Each *pop* of the seven buttons drew her nerves, and her nipples, tighter.

He shoved his jeans down and off his body, taking his socks off with them and then stood gloriously naked in front of her.

"Wow." Her mouth dried up. Flat, hard stomach with an enchanting line of hair leading to his very healthy equipment. Listing to the left. She liked that, liked how it'd felt inside her. Right then it was very hard. "I do so love a man with such a good recovery time."

He laughed but made no move to stop her as she took her time looking him over, taking in every inch of his body. Unable to stop herself, she skimmed her palms down his back and over his muscled ass. "This is even nicer unclothed."

When she reached his front again, his eyes were a deep, dark green and a very naughty grin had taken residence on his lips. A thrill worked through her at the sight of that face. Shit, she totally should have started doing younger men years ago. Even as she thought it, she knew it was a lie. It wasn't about his relative youth, it was about *him.*

"By the way? You're not overcompensating. Not at all."

Surprise overtook his features for a moment and he threw his head back to laugh. The floor swept out beneath her and she landed with a laugh on the bed, Marc looming over her.

"Did you like what you saw?"

"I like what I see very much. I'd like it even more if you got busy with all those arms and legs, your mouth and hands and that verra fine cock you've got there."

"On your hands and knees then. Face the other way. I want to fuck you from behind but this way I can see your face in the mirror. See you come with those beautiful cat eyes looking up at me so you don't forget who's bringing you such pleasure."

Holy shit, the man was lethal with the talking. Who knew? Ugh, again with the surprises. He was like the ultimate Pandora's box of naughty.

She moved quickly and he settled himself behind her. They were well matched height wise, his groin pressed against her ass and the back of her pussy.

But he didn't plunge in. Instead he bent and licked the length of her spine until a soft squeal of surprised pleasure came from her.

"I don't have any neighbors and the shoe store is closed. Feel free to make as much noise as you like." The edge of his teeth found her hip, biting her gently. "I just want to eat you up." He paused and met her eyes in the mirror. "Again."

She moaned as shivers of delight broke over her. She looked back, under the line of her body, watching as he sheathed himself.

"Now then." He pressed the head of his cock just inside her body and waited. One of his hands gripped her hip, keeping her from ramming herself back against him to take him inside. The other stole around her body and palmed a breast, moving to slowly tug and roll the nipple until she writhed as much as she could.

"Please!"

"Please what? Tell me what you want, Liv."

"Fuck me. Please. Stop teasing me and fuck me."

"My pleasure." He slid deeply into her in one strong push before pulling out nearly all the way.

If Marc hadn't already loved her, watching her as he fucked her would have sealed the deal. It took a lot of trust for a woman to let herself be taken from behind like that. More trust to tell a man what she wanted and then to receive it with utter erotic abandon.

Her breasts swayed as she moved back to meet his thrusts, soft sounds broke from her as he played with her incredibly sensitive nipples. She was wet and creamy and he'd never felt anything as good as being deep inside her. His fingertips found her clit again, coaxing her into another orgasm.

And when she came? Holy moley she looked absolutely luscious. Her face flushed, eyes glassy, lips wet from her tongue. He'd seen a lot of women orgasm, but this one was beyond compare.

He loved how easy it was to make her climax as well. Once when he'd gone down on her, another as he made love to her in the truck, a third time with his hands just moments before and now he'd have her do it herself.

"Liv?"

"Mmmmmm?" she responded, lazily, sexily, making him smile.

"I want you to make yourself come."

"I don't know if I can."

"Do it for me, Liv. I know you've got another in you, give it to me."

She hesitated a moment but keeping her eyes locked with his, slid her hand over her belly and her fingertips met the place where their bodies were joined.

Her eyelids slid halfway closed as she began to touch her clit and he watched, fascinated as the muscles in her arm and wrist corded and he felt the telltale flutters of the walls of her pussy around him.

Sweat broke out on his temples as he struggled not to come yet. He wanted her to go first but the carnality of what she was doing, the way she felt around him, the scent of their sex on the air beat at his control.

"Come, Liv. Come," he urged through clenched teeth as he quickened his pace, fucking into her harder and deeper. Climax gathered in his balls, in the soles of his feet and the top of his head.

Her head shot back and her eyes widened, catching his in the mirror. That luscious mouth opened in a silent howl and, as her orgasm exploded around his cock, his unleashed into her body in wave after wave of quicksilver pleasure until he had to collapse to the mattress, bringing her down with him.

"Be right back," he mumbled. When he walked back into the room she'd sat up and was reaching for her blouse. He jumped onto the bed, tackling her down with him.

"Where do you think you're going?"

"Well. Uh, home I guess."

"Oh I don't think so. I like you right here. It's late and I'm going to make you breakfast before I have you again in the morning."

"You don't seem the type to have women sleeping over. I don't want to ruin your reputation."

He moved to rest on one elbow, unable to resist leaning down for a kiss. "I didn't use to be the type, no. But I seem to be now. I want to wake up with your warm, sexy body ready for me."

"And do I have a say in the matter?" she asked acerbically and he stifled a grin.

"Always, darlin'. If you don't want to sleep over, I'll run you home right now. I'd never force you to do anything you didn't want to. But I would make it worth your while when you woke up."

Seconds ticked by as she lay there thinking and he only barely kept himself from flicking his tongue over those delicious nipples daring his control as they poked up toward the ceiling.

"Will you put cheese in the omelet you're going to make me? And real milk in my coffee?"

Ah, triumph! "Yes. I've got some ham too. Although the milk is skim, the beans are gourmet."

"Good because I don't skimp on breakfast and I don't go in for soy cheese or any of that crap. I want real cheese and real eggs, not that fake egg stuff and I don't want egg whites either."

"Now you're just being greedy." He kissed the tip of her nose and she laughed.

"I am greedy. I like to eat and eat well. I work out and watch what I eat but that doesn't mean I'm giving up the joys of eating pizza or omelets with egg yolks. And don't bother trying to tell me a pizza on whole wheat crust with no cheese is just as good because that's a bald-faced lie."

"You're a difficult woman. It's a good thing I want to sink into your body for weeks. Egg white omelets are just as good."

She made a face and he wanted to laugh. "That is such a lie. I gave up mayonnaise. Okay. I don't eat omelets everyday but when I have one, I'm having one. No halfway fake omelet. I want it all or what's the point of eating oatmeal five days a week?"

"You drive a hard bargain, Olivia Davis. You'll have your full egg omelet with cheese and ham."

"Then you'll have my warm and willing body to wake up with."

Sighing contentedly, he pulled her against his body and kissed her temple. "Wanna watch a movie?"

Chapter Six

Before the sun rose, Liv lay in Marc's bed, his arms around her and his heart beating softly against the ear she'd laid against his chest. She should have felt warm and relaxed. Instead she fought back a sweat of terror.

She was in over her head. The sex, oh man the sex had been incredible. Earth shaking. Hot, hard and deep in more than one way.

Never had she felt connected to a man during and after sex the way she had with Marc the night before. His hands on her body were an anchor, holding her to Earth when she wanted to float away.

She could not feel this way about him. She couldn't afford the emotional capital. The roar of the fear Matt had left in his wake echoed through her, filling every cell.

At the same time, she was frozen, laying there because she wanted him. Wanted him so much it scared her, but now that she'd had a taste she couldn't bear the thought of letting him go. It was monumentally stupid. It was monumentally selfish but she knew she wasn't going to walk away just yet.

Instead, she planned, tried to work out just exactly how she'd manage the situation and her intense attraction to the man at her side.

Until he woke up and decided to greet the day in a very inspired manner.

ಬಃಃಃಃ

"We need to talk about all this."

Marc looked up from his plate, across the table at a very warm, very satisfied Liv. "All this?"

"You and me. Last night."

He smiled. Okay then. It was going to be easier than he'd thought it would be. "All right."

"Clearly we've got some pretty major chemistry. I can't deny that. I can't deny the sex is amazing and that I'm in no major hurry to give it up."

"Good. I don't plan to give it up."

She waved it away. "But it makes sense to talk about our boundaries. Because as I said, I'm looking for something long term and you're not. So I think that we can continue with this until the attraction burns out and I'll also keep looking. If you find yourself attracted to someone else, just let me know and I'll step out of the way. There's no reason why we can't stay friends. We're both adults. Both sexually liberated. Let's enjoy our time and move on as friends when it's over."

His fork clattered to his plate and he saw red. "What the fuck are you talking about?"

"Language."

"Fuck language, I've heard you curse a blue streak. In fact, I heard it about twenty minutes ago when you ordered me to eat your pussy."

He should have been satisfied by her blush but he was too pissed off. "You think I should just service you while you look around for some man worthy of your forever, Liv? Is that what you're saying? I'm good enough to fuck but not good enough to be with on Christmas?"

"What? Why are you being this way? You're the one who has a flavor of the week on your arm. You're the one who's fucked every damned woman under thirty in this town."

"Thirty-five." The moment he said it he regretted it.

Her eyes narrowed and she put her fork down. "As you say, *thirty-four, thirty-five in a month.* In any case, you're the one who has the love em and leave em lifestyle. I've told you up front what I'm looking for. I haven't lied about that."

"Stop being so sensitive about your age. God. It's not a thing. And I told *you* up front that I'm wooing you. I want you, Liv. Not for the next week or two, but for the long haul. But if you don't think I'm good enough, you should go now."

"I never said that and I don't think that. Where do you get this good enough crap anyway? When did I say any such thing? I'm trying to be sensible. You're the one who nearly passed out when I said I wanted to get married."

"That was months ago and before I told you I wanted to woo you. Before I worked my ass off to show you I was not the same person I used to be. You've changed me, Liv. And I know I've changed you. Don't you fucking lie to yourself or me. The sex between us was spectacular. It wasn't like that with Matt or Brody or any of the other men you've burned through. It didn't work with any of them because you're meant to be with me."

She stood up and he did as well. "Burned through? Are you insinuating I'm a slut? Because pot, meet kettle."

"Oh ho! I never said any such thing. Burned through, as in you dated them and it didn't work out, you moved on to the next guy, same story. And are you saying I'm a slut?"

She closed her eyes and it looked like she was counting to herself. Suddenly his anger drained away and he wanted to laugh. Fear. She was afraid of what they had together and was spitting like a cat in a corner. He could handle that. He would have her in the end. He just needed to wait her out.

"I need to go before I say something I can't take back. I value your friendship more than I value the orgasms you can give me. Yes, it was amazing, but not worth losing you over."

She slid on her shoes and grabbed her bag but he didn't miss the way her voice trembled when she spoke about losing him.

"I'm not finished. Let's talk this out."

"I am. I'll see you Monday."

"For heaven's sake, Liv. You're not going to lose me! This is a dumb fight because neither one of us is being totally honest. I want you. In bed and in my life. You want that too. I know you do."

He saw confusion war with fear in her features.

He softened his voice. "At least let me drive you home so you don't have to do the walk of shame through town. We can talk about this again soon, when you've got your thoughts together."

The rigidity in her spine eased and he knew he'd won at least a small amount.

When he got her home, after they'd both ignored the heady scent of sex in his truck, he'd kissed her before she could scramble out the door. "I'm not going anywhere, Liv. Get it through your thick head. I'll see you tomorrow."

"Tomorrow?"

"Yes. My parents' for dinner. Momma's expecting you."

"I never said I'd go!"

He chuckled. "This is Polly Chase. You never said you wouldn't. When she told you she wanted to see you for dinner more often and you agreed, she took it that you were coming to dinner again tomorrow night." He was *so* lying on his mother and he'd have to go deal with her right then. He knew though, that Polly would be on his side in this battle. Liv would fall and he'd be there to catch her.

Liv sighed. "Fine. I'll see you tomorrow." She got out of the truck and he watched her until she'd gotten safely inside before heading over to his parents' house.

ဆဘဆ

Liv slumped into her house and moved straight to her bathroom. Turning on the taps of her great big old antique tub, she took her clothes off, trying to ignore Marc's scent but it was impossible. Because it was on her skin. Under her skin. In her hair and brain, on her tongue.

With a groan, she went to make herself a cup of coffee, turning off the taps when the bath had filled. Minutes later, she sank into the water and sipped her coffee. She did her best thinking in her bathtub.

He said he wanted her for the long term. But was it just the sex talking? They were friends so did he feel more hindered, less able to give her the truth about how he felt?

And the sex. Oh man, it was way more than just sex. He'd seared her soul deep. Her body had responded to his in a way that satisfied her but scared the hell out of her at the same time. So dominant and sure of himself sexually, the allure of that was overwhelming.

Giving up control to him had been the most liberating thing she'd ever done. If she'd done that with Brody would they still

92

be together? What about Matt? Did the men in her life leave because she was too much in control?

"I think too much," she mumbled as she put down her empty cup of coffee and slid beneath the surface of the water. The silence surrounded her as the water embraced her body. It was just her and her insecurities and fears.

She sat up and wiped her eyes. Most people saw her as supremely confident and self assured but beneath that were the doubts. Maybe she wasn't worthy of love. Maybe she wasn't meant to be cherished. It was her, she was the reason they all left. What had she done to chase them away?

The tip of something very powerful had surfaced in her time with Marc and it scared the hell out of her. A man like Bill didn't scare her. He was managed easily enough. Being in charge meant she controlled her feelings and he couldn't hurt her. A man like Bill was who she needed to marry.

Wasn't he?

ಐಓಐಂ

Polly rolled out biscuits in the kitchen and smiled to herself as she waited while the other line rang. A ham baked in the oven, scalloped potatoes bubbled, peas with pearl onions next to that, and baked beans simmered on the stove.

"Hello?"

"Olivia, hon, how are you today? I was just calling to double check that you liked ham."

Liv stuttered and it made Polly smile even more.

"Oh for dinner tonight? About that, I hadn't really..."

"You are coming, aren't you? I've made an awful lot of food and I'd be so disappointed if you didn't come. You said you would last week or did I get it wrong? I'm getting old you know, sometimes I suppose I misunderstand but I was just thrilled you said you'd come."

Liv sighed and Polly barely held back a laugh.

"Oh no, you didn't misunderstand. Of course I'll be there. I love ham. Can I bring anything?"

"Now you're just insulting me. Just yourself, honey. See you tonight." Polly hung up, chuckling to herself.

Her boy wanted Liv Davis, he'd have her. It helped that she and Edward adored Liv and she was already considered a member of the family. But what mattered to her most was another one of her children realizing what it meant to love someone. Truly love her.

Liv was wary and Polly couldn't blame the girl. After all, even Polly knew about Marc's reputation and that had to scare any woman. And after the thing with Matt failing, Polly knew Liv's heart would be wounded and she'd be careful of a man like Marc. And the girl had lost a lot in her life. Her mother at a young age, her sister had been a handful and her father had up and left to Florida ten years before. Aside from Maggie, Liv had been alone a lot.

Family meant everything to Polly and she'd pull out all the stops to make Liv part of theirs.

ಇಂಚಿಂಚ

"The woman is diabolical," Liv muttered as she pulled up next to the curb out front. She should have begged off, she knew that but it wasn't in her to refuse Polly "the amazing steamroller" Chase.

Marc had sent her an email the evening before. She'd ducked his phone calls but curiosity made her read the email. He'd just been checking in on her and he repeated that he wanted her for the long term and that he wasn't giving up or walking away.

She wanted to believe him but it scared her to contemplate trusting anyone that way. It was a huge risk. *He* was a huge risk. She'd be a fool to trust a man like Marc Chase when he said he wanted something long term.

He opened the front door and strolled down the front walk to meet her. She didn't even have time to give a surprised squeak when he grabbed her and laid a hard, long kiss on her out there in front of God and the neighbors. Not that she resisted, it felt too good after all her thinking. Eased the tension of fear in her gut. Replaced it with warmth and a pulsing, simmering desire. Again with the pushing of her buttons.

"Good evening, Olivia. This is a lovely outfit. Is it new?" He stepped back, leaving her slightly breathless but keeping an arm around her waist. Which was a good thing because her knees were rubber. She couldn't take her eyes off his thumb as it cruised over his bottom lip, clearing off her lipstick. She licked her lips in response and he got that wicked grin.

"Uh, yes. New. Just got it last week when I drove into Atlanta with Cassie for beads. Thank you."

He escorted her into the house and before she could gather her wits, half the family saw him with his arm around her and her lips kiss-swollen.

"Well, it's about time." Maggie laughed and kissed Liv's cheek. "Must have been some picnic. Don't think I don't know you've been ducking my calls. You're going to tell me every last detail," she murmured into Liv's ear.

"Uh."

Marc squeezed her, pulling her closer, and kissed her temple. "Everyone lay off. Miz Liv here is wary about me, and rightfully so. So if you rib her about this you'll be making my job harder."

Matt chuckled and kissed Liv's forehead. "It's going to be weird hearing all the details about my brother the way you shared about Brody. Although frankly, it's a big step up for you."

"Don't patronize me, Matt Chase." Liv narrowed her eyes at him and he chuckled more.

"Okay, sweet stuff. You got it. Although, you're fun to patronize, you have to admit."

"I'm gonna kick you in the junk," Liv muttered and shook Marc off, heading toward Cassie who accepted a hug and a kiss on her cheek without comment.

"Let's go into the sitting room and have a beer, shall we?" Maggie said brightly. "Well, you all can have a beer and I'll have a root beer." She sent a dark look back at the brothers gathered behind them. "No boys allowed."

Marc walked up and kissed her again, bold as you please before heading into the living room with his brothers to watch whatever game was on the nine hundred channels' worth of sports Edward had.

"Well! Okay, come on." Cassie pulled Liv into the sitting room. "Before Polly gets in here, she's on the phone, spill!"

Liv cracked open a beer and took several long swallows before tossing herself into a chair. "I am so in trouble."

Maggie laughed. "Looks like the best kind of trouble."

Liv told them about the picnic and afterward, ending with their fight the morning before.

"Give him a chance. What have you got to lose?" Cassie sat back, one eyebrow raised.

"My heart."

Maggie waved a hand around. "Olivia Jean, if you don't think I can't see you've already lost it, you're out of your mind. We've been friends a very long time. We've been through a whole lot together and you've been there for me when things were so dark I wasn't sure if I'd survive. Why don't you let me be the one supporting you for a change, okay?

"I can see it on your face, can hear it in your voice. You have deep feelings for Marc. It's way more than sex. You're falling in love with him. Why resist?"

"Look what happened when I didn't resist Matt."

Cassie sighed. "I wasn't here for that so I can't say what it was like for you at the time but I've seen both of you since and Liv, while you have occasionally looked like you wanted to take a bite out of Matt, and who doesn't, the boy has a set of abs that makes me all tingly every time he parades around shirtless in those damned cutoffs. You know, the ones that hang a bit low on his hips so his belly shows all the way down to…oh, well where was I?"

Maggie burst out laughing and Liv joined her.

"Oh yeah, so anyway, you haven't been pining for Matt. You've been pining to belong to something bigger than yourself. And heaven knows I felt that way too. But Marc? The way you talk about him, the way he looks at you, touches you, Liv, you're not alone in your feelings. He may be, have been, a huge flirt and skirt chaser, but he's honest. I've never known him to be deliberately hurtful and I've never heard a single one of the women he's dated say one negative thing about him. And you're a goner already. You're in love with Marc. It's not like you can unlove him. Give the guy a chance already."

"Oh for cripes' sake! I just had sex with him one time. Okay, uh," she paused, thinking, "five, no six times. But still, that doesn't equal love. I have plans. I'm not going to give up on my plans for the future because I had some awesome sex. I have a date with Rancher Bill next week. I'm moving forward."

Maggie just shook her head. "You're a hard headed woman, Liv. Always have been. I hope you know Marc isn't just going to let you run things."

"I've noticed his tendency to be domineering, yes. But he doesn't get to run me. I've given him my terms. He can accept them or not."

ཨཽ๛ᏐᏣ

Marc smiled as she tried to maintain her distance from him at dinner. His mother had placed the two of them side by side so she couldn't avoid that. The whole family had just accepted her as his girlfriend no matter what she tried to say and she'd finally let it go in frustration.

"You know, if you gave her the illusion of cooperativeness with this so-called plan of hers, you'd probably sneak in past her defenses." Edward took a sip of wine when Marc came back inside after he'd laid one hell of a good bye kiss on Liv at her car.

Marc loved the difference between his parents. Polly just spoke whenever a thought occurred to her, good or bad. But Edward didn't waste words so when he said something, Marc always listened.

"Go on, Daddy," Marc urged as he rocked back and forth in the old rocker near the fireplace. His brothers were sprawled through the room, all listening to their father.

"I see a lot of people in tense situations. A hazard of the job I suppose. But in the thirty-nine years I've been doing this, I've learned a lot about people when they're feeling threatened or are emotionally exhausted. They fight anything and anyone that offers a real depth of feeling or experience. Because it's frightening to give yourself to something bigger than you are. So they resist and resist and drive people away. Liv is the kind of woman who knows what she wants. In theory."

"I think she knows, Daddy. And I want to give it to her. She wants a white picket fence and a couple of kids, marriage, a mortgage. I've never wanted any of that stuff and she makes me want it with her. What I don't know is how to get her past her fears that I'm not real."

"What I mean, Marc, is that wanting marriage and love and a family is one thing. But truly opening yourself up to those things is another. In order to really love someone, you have to make yourself very vulnerable. So she's loved people who haven't been capable of loving her back in the way she deserves. It's sort of a self-defeating cycle but certainly not unique. It ensures her hurt, yes, but not the depth of hurt she'd suffer if she truly loved any of these men. And I don't mean to be hurtful, Matthew, but you're the same way. You seek these women who you know on some level aren't right so you don't have to risk truly loving anyone and getting your heart broken.

"If something is worth having, it's worth losing. But that's scary. You're a brave man, Marc. You're in love with her, aren't you?" Edward stared at his son with perceptive eyes.

Marc sighed and nodded. "I realized it Friday night. I've always liked her, thought she was pretty and funny, smart, successful. All the things I admire in a woman. But I think the love thing has been growing as I got to know her better. I'm sorry, Matt, I hope this is okay with you."

Matt shrugged. "It hurts a little. But really only because I couldn't feel what you do for her. She deserves to be loved and I know you'll treat her right. I want that too, you know, I really do. I just haven't met the right woman yet."

"You will." Edward winked at Matt before turning back to Marc. "So here's what I think about you and the lovely Ms. Davis. You say she's got this plan to find Mr. Forever?"

Marc snorted and nodded. "I am that guy!"

"Of course you are, son. And she knows that too. I saw the way she looked at you, the way she responded to your touch. But as I said, she's afraid to really risk herself so she'll want to pursue the easy man who'll never challenge her and try and keep you out of her heart. Let her." Edward put a hand up to silence Marc. "Let me finish. Let her go out with these bland men in her search. She's not going to find anyone, because you're it. And in the meantime, you get right under her defenses and by the time she figures it out, it's too late. You have nothing to fear from the likes of Bill and other men like him. Liv Davis needs to be taken in hand. Your momma needed that too."

Edward laughed at the sight of his sons' faces.

"What? I'm not *that* old, boys. Your momma is a willful creature and needs lots of space to do her thing. Needs a man who'll let her be herself and love that about her. I do. But she also needs a man who won't take any nonsense and pushes back when she gets cranky. Liv is that kind of woman and our Marc, although he tries to fool everyone with that easy going smile, is that kind of man. Aren't you, boy?"

Marc chuckled. "To be honest, Daddy, I never thought of it that way. I've never felt any compunction to be like that with a woman before I met Liv. But yes, I've learned a few things about myself in the last months and that's one of them."

"The truth is, not every woman is worth the effort. You've found your woman, Marc. Let your Liv think she's on the search for Mr. Right when you're right there under her nose. Give her a few weeks to get the picture and then close the trap. It'll be hard to let her go like that, but you know, I get the feeling it's all going to be a big charade for her. She's not looking for anyone but you. Patience and you'll win this through."

"You're more diabolical than Momma. How come I never figured that out?" Kyle asked.

Edward chuckled. "If I have to tell everyone how diabolical I am, how diabolical could I really be?"

Chapter Seven

"Okay, you and I are going out for coffee when you're done tonight. We have some talking to do," Marc murmured as Liv came out of the locker room to stretch and warm up.

"I don't suppose I get a say in this?"

"Nope. Now get working."

The infuriating man actually sauntered off to help another one of his clients while she warmed up.

It helped that she was distracted while she worked out. Sort of. Marc's presence was nearly overwhelming. He leaned over her and touched her like he had a right. At one point he even brushed his lips over her temple surreptitiously.

She went through her workout quickly and efficiently. He shadowed her, making sure she did everything right, adding some reps and extra weight to a few of her machines.

Liv saw he was speaking with another client when she'd finished her warm down and hurried to the back to change clothes. She really didn't want to talk to him. She was weak, she'd missed him and had looked forward to seeing him that evening. He'd also left a mug on her desk with some of the tea she often drank at The Honey Bear. How did he know? It touched her way more than she wanted to be touched. No one ever did that sort of thing for her before. He noticed things like that, little things, small things but things about who she was.

When she came back out he was locking the front door, standing next to the other one. He turned and crossed his arms over his chest. "Going somewhere?"

"I have work in the morning."

"Mmm. It's only seven. We can even have coffee at your place, save some time." He grabbed his bag and waited for her.

Sighing, she took his outstretched hand and they left.

"What did you want to talk about?"

"Your ridiculous idea of boundaries."

"Ridiculous?"

"Look, it's a crock and you're using it to hold me back. Okay, fine. Here's what I'm willing to do. You and I will continue to see each other, naked and clothed. I will continue to show you that *I* am this forever guy and you will date blandoids like Bill. At some point, you will have to admit you and I are it, and this silly charade can end. Then we can move forward with a relationship."

"And you?"

"What do you mean, sugar? I'll be pining away while you're out on the town." He winked.

"You're such an ass." She was unable to stop the upturn of her mouth into a smile. He was infuriatingly adorable. And very accommodating. It made her nervous.

He took her keys from her hand and unlocked her door, following her inside.

"I *am* an ass. But in this I'm right."

"And I suppose you'll be dating all the twinkies in town while I continue my serious plan to find love." It hurt even to imagine it.

He laughed. "Do you want me to? Liv, sugar, I don't like twinkies. I far prefer pie and cobbler. In any case, no, I won't be

103

dating anyone with creamy filling but you. Because I only want yours."

"You're such bad news." How could she resist? He was funny. He made her laugh and what did she have to lose anyway? She could keep him and keep the plan in place. And a small part of her wanted to believe his claim about wanting a relationship with her. Okay, a big part. The part that beat then, just for him.

"I am. I'm very bad. And so are you. I think you need a little discipline." He waggled his brows at her.

"Oh man. I'm in trouble," she mumbled just before sprinting out of the room with him on her tail.

Laughing, he yanked her clothes off when he caught up to her.

"Bathroom. I need to shower. I'm all sweaty." She tried to fend him off, giggling.

"I could lick you clean. You taste mighty fine. But we haven't showered together yet so I'm all for firsts. I'll lick you dry."

He pulled his clothes off and she sighed happily, turning around to run the water.

"Nice bathroom you've got. That's some tub. Next time I foresee a long bath together. I do like you wet."

Those blue green eyes went to deep, dark green. Shivering, she took in the long look up and down her body he gave her. His cock was hard and standing at attention. He pulled the door to the enclosure open and she stepped in, leaning back to get under the spray.

His hands, slick with soap, began to explore her body and she fell back into his spell. With his hands on her, she couldn't think about anything else but him so she stopped fighting and let go. It seemed with him, there was nothing but to let go.

Fingers rolled and tugged her nipples, over and over in a slow, sensual rhythm. The wall of his chest felt sure, strong as she leaned into him.

"Just an appetizer before the main meal," he murmured before nibbling her ear.

Still rolling and tugging, Marc moved his other hand down to find her clit, swollen and ready. With the same leisurely rhythm, he brushed his middle finger over it, building the pleasure bit by bit until she was blind with it, aching for release.

Pleasure sucked her under as she gasped. Climax roared through her body as her back bowed.

Muscles still jumping, she dimly registered movement as he turned off the taps. Warm and lazy, she dried off, watching the water roll down his body in rivulets over the hard-packed muscle.

"What's that smile for? Where's the bedroom?" He took her hand and she sashayed past, naked and satisfied, drawing him toward the end of the hall where her bedroom lay.

"The smile is because you look so good. And this is my bedroom."

Marc looked at her, bathed in the yellowish light of the streetlamp out front, dark hair wet and plastered to her head, only emphasizing the sexy shape of her eyes. Her body was mouthwateringly beautiful but what was most alluring was her comfort with her shape and size, the way she owned her sensuality and had no shame as she stood naked before him.

Her room was a lot like her. Simple, strong and straightforward. Deep blues accented by lighter blues colored the walls and bedding. No frilly stuff anywhere. Black and white photographs hung framed on the wall, southern landscapes if he guessed correctly.

A laptop sat on a desk in the corner and in the other corner a single, overstuffed chair, flanked by a low table with a lamp and an open book. The space smelled like her. Minty but also, he paused, thinking as he had so many times trying to identify it...coconut?

"Liv, sugar, what perfume do you wear?" he asked her as he nuzzled her neck, rubbing the entirety of his naked body against hers, walking her backwards to her bed.

"I don't wear perfume."

He liked the way her breath hitched before she could answer him.

"What's that smell then? Mint and is that coconut?"

She laughed as he pushed her back onto the bed. "Oh, that's the stuff I put on my skin. Coconut and mint. Smells delicious doesn't it? Oh, my!"

He teased the entrance to her pussy with the head of his cock. He'd never wanted to plunge into a woman without protection as he did at that moment.

"Condom? Please say you have one in here or I have to go back into your bathroom for my pants."

Stretching her arm out, not leaving his embrace, she opened a drawer in her bedside table and rustled around, holding up a foil package in triumph.

Within moments he sheathed himself and sank into her body with a groan. When he was inside her, it felt like home. It felt so good there, deep within her, he wanted to yell it out to the whole world.

Each breathy gasp, every moan and sigh and squeal she made shot straight to his cock. He made her feel that way, no one else. And no one else would.

He had no problems telling her she could date these other guys while she figured out he was the right one because he knew, despite her attitude, she wouldn't be with anyone else but him. No, what they had between them wasn't simply sex, not only sex, but the sex was part of it and she'd know it. Deep inside the way he touched her, the way he made her come would be there no matter what she did or who she was with.

It was a matter of seducing her heart because her body was his.

When he looked deep into her eyes, their faces just inches apart, he felt as if he were drowning in her. He kept returning to kiss her lips as he slowly thrust into her pussy over and over, taking in her breath as he captured her lips.

"You feel amazingly good," she gasped out.

"Yes, oh yeah. I feel good. You feel like heaven around my cock, Liv. I was made to be here, inside you."

He changed his angle, rocking back to push her knees up, opening her to his thrusts. He knew he had it perfect when he swiveled a bit, grinding himself over her clit.

"Ah, you've got another one in you, don't you, sugar? Give it to me." He wanted to give her pleasure, wanted to make her happy and fulfilled. And right then he was. He felt the first tense and flutter of her inner walls around him and her nipples hardened. A low moan tore from her.

"Come on, Liv, come. I can't until you do and I want to. I need to." He felt climax build and build, threatening to overflow and take over his system.

Arching her neck back, she rolled her hips to meet his thrusts and cried out as she came, pulling him down with her as he let go and orgasm rushed through him.

He continued to thrust until he was soft, finally rolling to the side.

Moments later, he pulled her into the curve of his body and kissed the top of her head.

𝕰𝕺𝕾𝕮𝕾

Liv woke up, warm and safe. Before she opened her eyes she knew why. Marc lay curled around her. As she wasn't fully awake she could admit to herself that it felt good.

Waking up with Brody never felt like that. Waking up with Matt never felt like that. Before thought fully returned, she snuggled into him, breathing in his skin, listening to the slow beat of his heart as she laid her ear against his chest.

He made her want to melt, made her feel feminine and soft. Vulnerable in a way she hadn't imagined she ever could. And yet, all that outer stuff was stripped away. She was who she was, no artifice, no bull and he stayed.

How long would that last? How long would he be all right with her dating other people and how long would he not do it too? He'd use her dating as an excuse to see other women too. And he'd be right to, after all she was. God, she'd built in her own damned self destruct for this thing. When it went bad, there'd be a reason, one she could accept.

She would just ride it out between them until she found the right guy and Marc was ready to move on. Hopefully, she'd find the right guy first because she was pretty sure her heart would break when he walked away.

She eased away from his sleeping body, standing next to the bed to look at him before she jumped in the shower to get ready for work. His face was partially hidden by strands of his hair. A morning shadow of beard covered his chin and cheeks, making him look sexily disheveled instead of messy.

Reluctantly she turned to go into the kitchen, start coffee and head to the shower.

He was sitting at her kitchen table, reading the newspaper when she came out, dressed for work.

"You look nice today." He smiled.

As the only thing he was wearing was a patch of sunshine across his shoulders, she thought nice was a relative term for what he looked.

"You look mighty sexy, Marc." His hair was wet and combed back away from his face, only highlighting the lines of his face. He had the kind of good looks that could sell men's sportswear and casual clothing. Boy next door with a healthy heaping spoonful of sin twinkling in his eyes.

He stood and kissed her, careful not to smear her lipstick.

"Are you late for work or anything?"

He shook his head. "Nope. I have a client in about forty-five. I go to her place though."

Liv took a sip of coffee and said nothing, although silly jealousy ran through her. She hated jealousy. It was a useless, base emotion and she should be above it. However, right about then all she wanted to do was let this mysterious client know Marc woke up in her bed that morning. *Hmpf.*

Marc smiled as he watched her face change. Ah, jealousy. And not the petty kind that he'd experienced from women before. She didn't pout or throw a tantrum. But she had started to think of him as hers on some level. *Good*. He sure as hell knew she was his.

She was so beautiful and sexy, watching her move through her kitchen, getting herself breakfast—after asking if he wanted any—with that pretty, bright red dress floating around her legs made him crazy. He wanted her. No, he *needed* her. Thinking that other men would see her and have naked thoughts about his woman made him edgy. He'd never actually been jealous before. It was another indicator that he loved and adored this woman. Or something.

"What's that smile for? Makes me nervous," Liv sat across from him and ate her oatmeal.

"It should make you nervous. I was thinking about waking up next to you on Christmas morning with my mother yelling up the stairs for everyone to get their lazy butts out of bed and get downstairs for breakfast and presents."

Okay, so he shouldn't have enjoyed her reaction to that so much but it did make him chuckle. Because she *would* be there for Christmas, next to him, opening presents and eating breakfast with his family. She belonged with him and there was nothing else that could convince him otherwise.

"You're skittish. Like one of those little dogs. Never know when you're going to go off and snap at me. My client this morning is Lula Parsons. She's heartier than her seventy years yes, but you're way hotter." He winked, just to poke at her more.

"Marc Chase, I do believe you enjoy fucking with me."

"I enjoy fucking you, yes. A lot. More than I've enjoyed anything. Ever. It's not generally what I mean when I say your insides are beautiful, but that's part of it."

She blushed, touching him deeply. Had no one ever really complimented her? Made her feel special? It wasn't like Matt to not treat the woman he dated with extra care but clearly she seemed uncomfortable and unused to it. Maybe it was him. He'd need to think on it more, watch her reactions. But he planned to put Liv on a pedestal and treat her like a queen because she deserved it.

She stood and put her dishes in the sink. "I'm going to get on. Lock up when you're ready to go."

"Oh hang on, let me walk with you."

She leaned against the sink, watching him as he pulled on his clothes.

"Wait a sec." She went into her bedroom and came back out a few moments later. "I can't help you with underwear. Not that I want to, I like knowing you're naked under there. But here's a pair of gym socks and a clean T-shirt. It's way too big for me but it should fit you."

Smiling he took the shirt and pulled it over his head and got the clean socks on. The dirty stuff went into his bag. He hadn't the heart to tell her he had clean shirts and underwear in the messenger bag. He liked wearing something of hers. If they were hers.

"Hey, whose clothes are these?"

"Mine, silly. The shirt was some contest win and they just gave everyone extra-larges And everyone has gym socks don't they? Do you think I'd be so tacky as to give you some other man's clothes?"

He laughed. "No. I don't think you're tacky. I think you're fabulous."

They walked hand in hand to city hall and parted ways at the front steps with a quick kiss. He liked that she didn't shy away from the public affection and he really liked the sway of her ass as she took the steps toward the front doors.

"Saucy." Grinning, he turned and jogged toward his place.

Chapter Eight

Friday night some weeks later found Liv staring at him as he played pool. And the damned little chickies who seemed to follow him around everywhere.

"It sucks. Just get used to it now."

Liv looked back at Maggie. "What are you talking about?"

Maggie snorted. "Puhleeze. Girl, don't you play coy with me. I've watched this thing blossom between you and Marc. You're watching him with hungry eyes right now. But you see the fan club too. Chase brothers come with a fan club. You're going to have to accept it. If you let it agitate you, you're going to be agitated all the time."

"I'm not agitated."

"Yeah, I can tell. Olivia Jean, you have got to stop lying to yourself or this is never going to work. All these women can do is look. He's not doing a thing to lead them on, not giving them any attention other than a how do you do."

"Don't you let this silliness hold you away from something real with him. Speaking of silliness, how'd the date with Rancher Bill go?"

Liv turned to Cassie, ready to be upset but just let out her breath in a sigh. "Fine. I don't think we'll have any more dates."

"What? I mean aside from the fact that you're in love with Marc and all?"

"You're on a roll tonight aren't ya, California girl? Sheesh."

"It's July again. I freaking hate July in Petal. It's so *hot.* Makes me pissy."

Liv laughed. "Not as hot as August."

"I hate August even more than July. But there are plusses to August. Nice parties. Thank goodness we have good air conditioning. Back to Rancher Bill?" Cassie's face was amused as she munched on her fries.

"He's a nice guy but he's not right for me. He doesn't do anything for me physically. It's not like he's bad or anything, he's just got no moves."

"You had sex with him?" Maggie's mouth dropped open.

Liv's eyes went wide, offended. "No. I'm having sex with *Marc.* I'm not a skank. Jeez. But I wasn't even tempted. I mean, he can't be Mister Right if I'm not even tempted can he? I don't think so."

"Is that the new standard then? If you feel like tossing Marc out of bed for him, that's the dude? Sounds pretty crass, Liv. Oh, I know! How about you just stop this and admit Marc is Mister Right?"

"A few years in town and you're suddenly all uppity," Liv grumbled into her beer.

"I was uppity before I came to Petal." Cassie laughed.

"It's why I like you so much. Anyway, Bill and I had a talk at the restaurant."

Maggie's eyes widened. "Really now? What about? He didn't ask you to marry him?"

Liv laughed. "No."

As a matter of fact, she and Bill had been sitting there at dinner, drinking some wine and listening to the piano music when he'd looked her straight in the eye and said, "This can't work, you know."

"What do you mean?"

"Liv, I like you an awful lot and you're nice to me. Sweet. I like your laugh. Sexy even. But you're in love with Marc Chase. Any fool could see it."

She'd nearly choked on her wine then. "What? He and I are friends. We date. I'm not in love with him."

Bill laughed then. "Olivia, one of the most attractive things about you is how straightforward you are. Blunt. You're take charge, you don't play games like other women do. But if you can't see you're in love with the man, you're not as straightforward as I thought. Or maybe you're defending your heart so hard you can't see your nose to spite your face. Is that it?"

Liv wished then that she'd been attracted to him. He was compassionate and smart. But not Marc. Damn. He was right.

He'd waited, watching her as she scrambled to process what he'd said, trying to deny it.

He smiled a bit sadly. "I do wish you and I had something because you're going to make Marc a fine wife. He's a lucky man. You're beautiful but scared aren't you?"

"I'm a big girl. I am, however, sorry if I led you on. I truly wanted it to work. You're attractive, smart, good. You're a very good man. But I don't know if I can overcome my really questionable taste in men. I seem to have a terrible addiction to men who are never going to make a commitment to me."

Raising a glass to her he shook his head. "As much as I'd like to run Marc down, I've seen the way he looks at you. The man is in love with you, Olivia. You're not like the other women

115

he's squired around. But if he hurts you? I'll be here. After I kick his ass."

He'd taken her home and she'd cried herself to sleep.

But she didn't tell Cassie and Maggie any of it because she was afraid to say it out loud. Afraid to believe it could be real.

"He knew we weren't right for each other. He was very nice about it. But as I keep telling you both, this thing with Marc and me is just a nice fling. He's a wonderful friend and I like him a lot. The sex is amazing but we all know he's not the forever type."

"No matter how many times you say that, Liv, it's only you who thinks so. I watch Marc with you every Sunday, every Friday and I think he looks an awful lot like a man who's invested in forever. I've never pegged you for a woman who would go out of her way to avoid happiness. It's sort of annoying because you're damned smart." Cassie looked over and her face lit up as Shane waved. "That's my cue. I'm going to go kick their asses at pool. Maggie, honey, you're looking pale. Go home and rest." Cassie kissed Maggie's cheek.

"My due date isn't for two weeks now. I don't want to pull Kyle away from his game."

Liv rolled her eyes at Cassie who shook her head. "You're full term now they said. I didn't go to all those birthing classes and watch those films of women squatting while giving birth to have you ignore your health."

"The shower is tomorrow anyway. A full day with Polly, you'll need the sleep." Cassie winked.

"You're right. Okay."

"I'll send Kyle over and I'll see you tomorrow," Cassie called over her shoulder as she headed back.

Marc watched his sister-in-law approach. "Damn, Shane, your wife is something else."

Shane smacked him on the head with his cue. "Knock it off."

Cassie stood on tiptoes to kiss Shane and looked around him to Kyle. "Take your wife home. She's exhausted and the shower is tomorrow."

"Is she okay?"

The panic in Kyle's voice tore at Marc. Loving someone that much, so much that you worried for their health and now the health of the life she carried used to scare him. But despite the fear, Marc saw the glow about his brother too.

Cassie touched Kyle's arm gently. "She's fine. But she's thirty-eight weeks pregnant, hon. It takes a lot of energy to gestate and it's hot. Take her home, have her put her feet up and make sure she keeps drinking water. I'll see you tomorrow."

Kyle put his cue away and said his goodbyes. Marc watched him scoop his wife up with gentle arms and a smile on his face.

An ache built inside him and suddenly this whole thing with him playing along with the looking for Mister Forever seemed utterly stupid. He wanted to be with Liv full time.

Rocking back on his heels a moment, he zeroed in on the object of his thoughts. "Well lookit my girl over there. She'll be all by her lonesome soon. I best get on over and give her some company." Marc looked at Liv and when her gaze met his, he felt the connection to his toes.

"So she believe you yet?" Matt asked.

"I'm working on it. I hear she had a date with Bill on Wednesday. Worked out with me, even let me kiss her goodbye and went on a date with that dullard." That hurt.

"Marc, she didn't even let him touch her. She said there'd be no more dates with him. She broke it off. This whole thing is stupid. I've never seen her like this but she's afraid. So afraid."

Cassie reached out and touched his cheek. "I'm amazed you're doing this, I truly am. And I admire that you're giving her this space. But when Maggie asked if she'd had sex with Bill, Liv got pissed. Said she was having sex with you and what did Maggie think she was?" Cassie kissed his cheek. "Hang in there. She'll see. It's right in front of her face and for what it's worth, you've got no competition. This thing with Bill was just a way to keep from admitting it to herself. But he's out of the picture now as an excuse."

"Oh hell, I know that. I just don't like her lying to herself. I want to be with her. This is all a waste of time."

Cassie shrugged. "If she's worth it, you'll wait. Only you can decide if she is or not. Everyone has their limits."

He looked back over at Liv as she blew a kiss at Maggie, smiling. She was worth it. God he loved her. Okay, a little while longer.

"Night all," he called over his shoulder as he walked through the restaurant toward her. She turned to see him coming toward her and stood, waiting.

"Hi there, handsome."

Without a word, he pulled her to him and kissed her. Hard and possessive. Satisfaction settled into him as she melted into his embrace, opening her mouth to him.

He took his time, knowing that people watched them. Wanting them to all understand how it was. Liv Davis was his woman.

When he was finished he dropped a small kiss on the tip of her nose and each eyelid. "Hi yourself, gorgeous. You ready to let me rock your world?"

Great googly moogly. He'd been rocking her world since he dropped that kiss on her in April. Hell, she'd been an independent woman in charge and she could only manage to hold onto him as he'd turned her knees to rubber as he did every time he touched her.

"Let's hit it, shall we?"

He snared her with his gaze and she let herself be swept up, nodding. Grabbing her hand, he drew her outside. Down the block he paused and pulled her into an alley. Pushing her back against the wall, he ducked his head, his mouth finding hers again.

The wall, still warm from the sun, scratchy against her skin, dug into her back as he plundered her mouth. Deep in the shadows, his hands roved her body as her mind spiraled. She should not be doing this! But it felt so good. It was dark, no one could see and all he was doing was kissing her. His tongue, clever and carnal, slid along hers, his teeth nipped her bottom lip.

The humid evening air cooled the sweat on her skin as he pushed the bodice of her dress open and his hands found her breasts.

"No bra. God, what you do to me," he murmured, lips against the skin just below her ear.

Her hands slid down the wall of his chest to the waist of his jeans, unsnapping and unzipping them. She took him in her hands, sliding her grip up and down and he groaned.

His fingertips found the loose material of her dress and slowly pulled it up, exposing her thighs, and then he reached up the last inch and slid his fingertips into her panties.

She froze a moment until he brushed her clit and all thought left her. A rhythm of rolling hips, of thrusts and moans caught them, slowing time, taking them to another place where it was just the two of them.

"You're so damned sexy, sugar. I need you to come for me."

She whimpered softly as her thighs began to tremble. His cock in her hand was slick from the heat and the pre-come at the slit.

"Fuck. I'm so close. One touch and I'm halfway there with you. What do you do to me, Liv? So much, so much to me. You're so hot, so wet. I'm going to fuck you standing up when we get back to your house. I want to look in your eyes," he murmured into her ear, the heat of his body on her neck.

Liv had to bite back a scream when he pressed two fingers inside her and caught her where shoulder met neck, between his teeth. Orgasm came then, quicksilver, and she felt his warmth on her hand as he came as well.

With a soft kiss he rearranged her panties and let her skirt fall as his other hand pulled her bodice back together.

"Wait." She dug in her purse with trembling hands and pulled out a handkerchief, passing it his way.

He put it into his pocket when he finished. "I'll uh, get this back to you later in the week."

Smiling, she tucked his cock back into his jeans but let him button and zip to avoid any injury.

She should feel bad. He'd just made her come in an alley. But she didn't feel cheap, she didn't feel bad. The way he touched her was always respectful, he made her feel beautiful. The frenzy made her feel desirable.

"You make me lose control, Liv."

They continued to walk down to her house.

"Seems to me you have plenty of control, Marc." She laughed. "You're the most in control man I've ever been with.

Usually I'm the one in charge. You shoot that all to hell with your dirty talk and your swagger. You make me melt."

Holy crap, did she just say that out loud?

He turned to her, putting his arms around her shoulders. "Sometimes I feel like I'm a fool to keep chasing you. And then you give me a glimpse inside and I know you're worth it."

"Why do you say stuff like that?"

"Because I want you to know that I care about you. This isn't a casual thing for me, Liv. I don't know how many other ways I can say it to you."

He scared her. What she felt for him scared her. But she wasn't willing to let go just yet.

"Come on inside. I think you made a promise to me back in that alley that I need fulfilled."

೩೦ಔಎಉ

The next morning she awoke to find him up already. Sleepily, she shuffled into the kitchen to find him there, drinking juice and looking out the window.

"Morning, sugar." He turned and moved to kiss her.

"You off somewhere?"

"I have a client this morning. I'll see you this afternoon at the end of the shower when I'm told men are allowed. Not that I'm in any great hurry to guess baby food flavors and hear labor stories."

Liv laughed. "You think *I'm* in a hurry to hear labor stories? Dee's gonna be there and she and Maggie talk of little else. But I can't wait for Maggie to see the quilt I made for her. Took me six months."

Marc's eyes widened in surprise. "You quilt?"

"Why do you look so surprised? I can quilt, knit and cook quite well. When my mother was alive, she taught me all the things she thought a Southern woman should know. I can make a cobbler, mighty fine pie crust, scratch biscuits, embroider, quilt and a most excellent gravy."

"You're full of surprises, Liv. Wonderful surprises," he added quickly. "I'm impressed. I didn't know you were making it."

"It's something I do in the late evenings when I can't sleep and sometimes on my lunch hour I do the piece work. I just finished it a few days ago. You can see it this afternoon. I had Cassie wrap it because she's a pro at that stuff. My presents never look all crisp and pretty like hers do."

"I'm sure Maggie will love it."

"I hope so. Maggie is special to me. She's been my best friend since kindergarten. Not many people have relationships that last that long. She's always been there when I needed her."

He reached out and ran his fingertips through her hair. "From what I've seen, you've done the same for her. And Cassie too."

She rolled her eyes. "I don't bake for the elderly and teach kids to love history. I'm an administrative assistant."

Marc's chest tightened for a moment. He knew what it was like to love people who were all overachievers. His father the town lawyer, his brother the sheriff, the other brothers men the community looked to and admired. He was the baby. The always smiling man about town with an eye for the ladies.

"You're so much more than your job. And from what I see, you're the mayor's right hand. You seem to be better briefed than he is on things at town hall and city council meetings. And don't think I haven't seen you volunteering at the soup kitchen and food pantry. You're a good person and a wonderful friend and I'm more fascinated by you every day."

Leaning in, he brushed his lips over hers.

She blushed and he grinned. "Thank you. Is this a new client? You're doing really well these days. Can I make you breakfast? I'll even scramble egg whites for you."

Why that made him want to propose to her he wasn't sure.

"I am doing well. I'm at the point where I have to stop taking one on one clients just now. I'm working six days a week and the studio is full all day and into the evenings. And sure, I'd love some eggs."

She turned and began to assemble the eggs. He watched as she moved efficiently through the kitchen. He liked her house a lot. It was comfortable and lived in. He didn't feel wary about sitting down or using a plate or cup.

Her kitchen was bright and sunny from a large garden window over the sink. The scent of fresh herbs laced the air and he realized that it was a cook's kitchen. He'd cooked very simple fare for her a few times and she'd done sandwiches and salads but neither of them had made a dinner for the other yet.

"Will you make me dinner tonight?"

She tipped the eggs into the skillet and turned to him, smiling. "Sure. I'd love that. I can't believe we haven't yet. But it can't be tonight. Kyle and Maggie are having a barbecue at their place, remember?"

"Oh yeah. Okay. Well can't be tomorrow or my mother would hunt us down."

They agreed on Wednesday of the following week and he left after eating the eggs and some fresh fruit she'd sliced up for the both of them. Her kiss tasted like peaches and sunshine and he hated to have to go.

On the other hand, he was even more sure he loved her and that they belonged to each other. It strengthened his resolve to keep on with his plan.

‿◦◦‿

Liv showed up at Cassie and Shane's a few hours early to decorate for the shower. Smiling. Man oh man did waking up to Marc make her happy.

"Wow. That must have been some night last night." Cassie came back into the living room after she'd shooed Shane out of the house. "Spill. Polly will be here in a few minutes."

Liv laughed as she reached up and pinned the end of the twisted streamer. "You think they'll all figure out it's a boy when they see all the blue?"

Cassie took up her end and pulled it taut before pinning it across the room. "Maggie said that's what she wanted and I have no problem throwing her ass in front of me if Polly flips out."

"Man, you two have one of the best mothers-in-law ever. But you wouldn't want to cross her."

"She's wonderful and we *are* lucky. She's a good woman and she cracks me up. Nosy as hell and protective of her family. Can't complain about that one though."

They moved furniture and put out the cute little decorations they'd picked up the week before.

"Let's put the food over here and hello, you did not tell me about why you're smiling. You're sneaky all the sudden. With Brody you would not shut up about the details but with Marc it's like pulling teeth. I figure that means he's the real deal."

"Boy you're on that tune again. Okay here's the deal, Marc is special. I feel way out of my element and in over my head. I think..."

"Hey there girls! I've got the cake."

Cassie threw her hands up in the air. "Hold that thought. Don't think I won't be back to it," she called back over her shoulder as she moved to the front of the house where Polly had just entered.

The cake was gorgeous and the day was hot. They'd set up inside but had chairs and umbrellas on the deck as well if people felt up to it.

Polly helped them put the finishing touches around the place just before the guests began to arrive. Many faces, friends and family, filled the room, laughing and preparing to share the day with Maggie, who was set to arrive at any moment.

Liv directed people to the present table and to the food while Polly took in the blue decorations with a serene smile.

Kyle yelled from the front door when he dropped Maggie off. He'd been told to go away by Polly, who escorted Maggie into the room.

Dee had arrived earlier and was firmly in charge of the shower games. Liv just did what she was told and handed out clothes pins and carried the baby food jars on a tray for the smelling game. She sucked at both but it was fun anyway.

"Hey, Maggie, you want to go outside?" Liv asked a few hours in. "We've set up some shady seating areas."

"Girl, I weigh nine hundred pounds and have a nuclear heater in my belly. I'm not going outside until after the birth except to move to another air conditioned place," Maggie replied from her seat on the couch, her feet up and a smile on her face.

"Nine hundred pounds. Yeah, you're not overstating or anything. Can I get you some more juice?" Liv called to her as she moved to the table where bottles of juice nestled in ice.

Maggie sighed. "Between you and Cassie, I'm having to pee every five minutes."

"You need the liquids. You're a big baby. Go on and hit the bathroom and when you come back we'll do presents and you can have more juice." Cassie winked and Liv laughed. Having friends like the two of them meant so much to her.

Liv helped Maggie up from the couch and bustled around to get the presents ready for opening.

The room erupted in squeals as Dee took the clothes pin from Cassie's sleeve. "You said the forbidden word!"

Liv had lost her clothes pin an hour before and she couldn't guess any of the green baby food flavors. Truth be told they all stank to high heaven and Liv wouldn't have blamed any baby for refusing to eat it.

Maggie came back into the room and Liv pressed a fresh glass of juice in her hand before putting her in the present chair that happened to be a glider rocker, a gift from Matt.

"This is like the one I want for the nursery. Make sure to show it to Kyle when the boys get here."

"The boys are here," Kyle said as he entered. After looking around the room he glanced at Maggie with a raised eyebrow. "So you want to tell me something?"

"It was her idea," Cassie said quickly and Shane bent to kiss the top of her head.

"You're so eager to toss me under the bus, Cassie." Maggie said with a laugh. "You said I could tell you when I was ready. I'm ready now."

Kyle grinned. "A son it is apparently. I guess it won't be Sophia then, hmm?"

"Not this time."

Marc came in with Matt and made a beeline for Liv. The man certainly didn't hesitate to lay sugar on her in front of the entire room.

"Hi. You look pretty today."

He was utterly incorrigible and it worked for him. It worked for her too. She kissed the cleft on his chin. "Sit down, it's present time."

"Where are you sitting?"

She pointed to her chair and he pulled one next to it. She couldn't deny how flattered and pleased she was.

"Okay first of all, you don't need to show Kyle the rocker so he can buy one just like it. That's Matt's present."

Maggie laughed delightedly and held her hand out to Matt who came to kiss her and deliver a hug.

"No standing," Liv admonished Maggie. "Everyone has to come and give Maggie kisses like the princess she is. In fact." Liv bent and pulled out a tiara from behind the couch, meeting Cassie's amused eyes for a moment. "Here." She put the tiara on Maggie who simply grinned like a happy fool.

"I hope you all know I'm going to wear this all the time. Now presents!"

Liv laughed and she and Cassie began to bring presents to Maggie. There was much oohing and aahing over each little pair of pants and shoes, every little rattle and educational thingamabob. Polly, who'd been delighted instead of angry about finding out the gender of her first grandchild, would show Maggie and Kyle the nursery at her house the next night at dinner. Of course she couldn't resist just a few little things.

Which turned out to be a three foot high pile of outfits, booties, hats and other baby gear.

Penny arrived late, apologizing for the delay. They'd hit a huge traffic jam. She'd brought Ryan and baby Laurel.

"Grab some food and have a seat. We're nearly done with presents." Liv kissed their friend and that sweet two month old baby girl. "I call dibs on this baby when I'm done handing out presents."

Penny laughed. "You got it. I'll try and hold Polly off."

Liv handed the last package to Maggie after Penny got settled. "This one is from me."

Maggie tore into the beautifully wrapped package with glee and stopped when she saw the quilt. Carefully she pulled it out and looked it over.

"Oh my goodness. Liv, you made this. For me, for my baby." Maggie's voice was thick with emotion as she looked at the blanket.

"I did." Smiling, Liv pointed to the corners. "These two corners are made from Kyle's baby clothes and the top are from yours. Your daddy actually braved your mother to go and get them."

Tears in her eyes, Maggie stood and hugged Liv tight as she cried. "This is the most beautiful present I've ever gotten. Our son will sleep with a bit of his parents keeping him warm. And part of his Auntie Liv too."

Kyle hugged her as well. "Thank you, Liv. This is amazing."

"Stop it now, you're going to make me cry. Oh, there's a patch on the other side."

Maggie resettled back in the chair and turned the quilt over. The patch had the date it was finished and a little inscription. *Never doubt you're loved.*

"Sweet heaven, you've reduced an entire room to tears." Marc stood, putting his arm around her waist.

"I would have put his name there but I know you'll change your mind after delivery so I left that off. I'll add it later." Liv knelt beside Maggie.

"You're the best friend anyone could ever ask for. I don't have a very good biological family but I do have wonderful sisters of my heart in you and Cassie and soon," she rubbed her stomach and took Liv's hand, placing it over the place the baby kicked and squirmed, "another person to love. I'm so lucky."

Liv smiled, happy that Maggie had loved the quilt as much as Liv had loved making it for her.

Marc helped Liv up and Polly had Edward and Matt load all the loot into the car. Liv gave Maggie a piece of cake before turning to Penny and grabbing the baby.

Laurel had her daddy's coloring, pretty, big brown eyes and a shock of brunette hair. Her warm little body snuggled into Liv's and that sense of soft happiness stole over Liv. She may not be able to tell the difference between green beans and peas in a jar but she knew without a doubt she wanted this for herself.

Liv walked around and visited as she gently swayed back and forth with Laurel in her arms as Marc just watched.

"You want that." Polly handed him a soda and kissed his cheek.

"I do."

"With Olivia?"

"Without a doubt."

"Well, get working. I saw the way she looked at you when you came in. The way she leaned into your hug. That girl loves you."

"And I love her."

Polly grinned. "Have you told her?"

"Not yet. I'm afraid to scare her away."

"Too late for that. Go make me some more grandbabies."

Marc laughed even as he felt the pull in his balls as he watched Liv holding that baby. It matched the pull at his heart.

He moved to her even without realizing it, wrapping his arms around them both, pressing a kiss to her neck.

"Hey there, Laurel Ann," he said softly, loving the way the baby's eyes moved from Liv's face to his. "This baby sure is a pretty one. You and Ryan done good." He winked at Penny, who blushed. Marriage looked good on her. He knew she'd been devastated when she lost her first husband but she'd moved on and found a new life with Ryan and this baby.

"Your momma keeps sending me looks, I'm gonna have to give her up soon." Liv leaned her head into his shoulder.

Oh how he wanted to say that they could have their own baby, but he didn't want to spook her. That afternoon he'd put a stamp on their relationship in a public way in front of their friends and family and she hadn't resisted. That was a huge step. He'd save the baby talking for after he told her he loved her.

He loved how she tended to her own people. How she took care of Maggie, making sure she rested and kept her feet up. The quilt with Maggie and Kyle's baby clothes had nearly done him in. She'd given Maggie and his brother a piece of her heart to cover their child in. She'd reached out to Cassie in the aftermath after her ex-husband had turned up in town and tried to kill her. Liv still cared about Matt even though he'd broken her heart. She was good people and he couldn't love anyone better.

He also knew his newest client had come from her referral. Several of his clients had. She took care of him, too, in her own way. With her referrals and scrambled egg whites. She kept nonfat milk in her fridge and berry sorbet instead of ice cream. She understood that his feelings about fitness weren't based on vanity but a desire to help people live healthy and long. She got him. No, not his love of her, she had a blind spot there but he understood why more and more each day. But she saw what was special about him, made Marc understand himself better and that was more than he could say about just about anyone else he knew.

"You're incredible," he said into her ear and she smiled.

"Thank you. Where did that come from?" She turned to him, still swaying with Laurel in her arms, the baby's eyes drooping heavily with sleep.

"You just being you. Can I give you a ride over to Kyle and Maggie's later?"

"I drove here but if you want to follow me back to my house, I'll ride with you from there."

He touched his forehead to hers. "You got it. Now give that baby to my momma before she explodes."

Liv rolled her eyes and snorted. "I know, I know. She's shown a lot of restraint actually. I suppose I should reward that."

He watched as she moved to his mother and handed the pink bundle over, catching sight of one bare foot as Laurel settled into his momma's arms.

"So does Liv know you love her?" Penny asked.

"She'd have to be blind not to," Ryan added.

"I haven't told her yet. She likes to pretend she's convinced I'm just Mister Right Now and she wants to find Mister Right.

But she's not taking that very seriously anymore. I'm with her five nights a week. She doesn't have much time to date." He snorted.

"She'll come around. Her heart's had some major beatings to it. Makes a girl scared of something real." Penny shrugged.

"I know. I'll be there when she finally figures it out."

"That's the kind of love any woman would be proud to have, Marc." Penny kissed his cheek.

Polly looked up at Liv as the girl finally handed that baby over. It made her heart skip a beat when she'd seen Marc standing close to Liv while she'd held the child. A vision of their future for a brief moment. Another one of her children had found his heart.

"Stingy is what you are." She winked. "Although with this little sugar plum, it's easy to be. Don't you just love the way they feel? Mmm, I miss holding babies. I can't wait until my grandson comes along."

"By the looks of Maggie's belly, that's going to be soon."

Polly chuckled. It was so easy, bringing these women into her family where they belonged. "True enough. You and Marc are going to make some pretty babies too. You do want babies don't you?"

Liv blinked several times and swallowed. Polly knew the girl couldn't overcome how she was raised and politeness was a weapon Polly would use without hesitation.

"Well, sure I want children someday. I don't know if Marc does but we're just dating casually. It's early to talk about children."

"Casually." Polly rolled her eyes. "Girl, you think I'm blind? I see the way you two look at each other." She waved it away.

"You keep lying to yourself but it's plain to me and anyone else with eyes. My son cares about you. It's about time you stop this silly charade that only hurts you both."

Liv sighed but didn't try to argue. She was tired of arguing when she knew everyone else was right. She wasn't dumb, nor did she have much talent at self denial. But damned if she knew what that meant.

She cleaned up in a daze but her heart knew exactly where Marc was the entire time.

Kyle and Maggie left for their house to get the barbecue going. It would be Maggie's way of thanking everyone for all they'd done although Liv had no idea where she'd put any more food after eating so much at the shower.

Back at her place, she changed while Marc replaced the lock on her back door. The key had broken off in it a few weeks before and he'd insisted on fixing it when he found out about it.

"I like you here, fixing things in my house," she said from the doorway before she thought better of it.

He turned and looked at her warily. "I like it too. This is a nice house. I like being here. It's impressive that you own your own home."

She shrugged. "I don't have any debts but this place. I have a decent income. My car was a frivolous impulse buy three years ago but I worked overtime to pay it off in three years instead of five. I can't see paying rent if I can pay to buy instead."

"What if this mythical Mister Right doesn't want to live here?"

She took a deep breath and leapt into the scary abyss. "Well, I can be flexible about living arrangements. But I don't think an apartment above a shoe store is better than my house."

A smile broke over his face as he moved to her. "You saying what I think you are?"

"I don't know. What do you think I'm saying?"

"That you finally believe I'm Mister Right and I'm here for the long haul."

"Do *you* believe that?"

He brushed his thumb over her lips. "I've believed that for months."

She took a deep breath. "Yes. I believe it. I'll pull my profile from the computer dating services today. Not that I have time to date when I'm with you all the time."

"You found time to date Bill."

"I'm sorry if I hurt you. I am. And it means so much to me that you didn't just walk away when I insisted on continuing to date. I don't even know what to say other than that I had to believe it, Marc. Bill was never a threat to you. I never even kissed him after you and I started up."

He kissed her softly. "It was hard, Liv. I know he wasn't a threat. If I'd believed otherwise I probably wouldn't have agreed to wait while you finally took me seriously. Still, I was worried you'd never see me and my intentions as genuine. What finally convinced you?"

She shrugged. "I don't think it was one thing. More a combination. Today at the shower your mother was the dozenth person to tell me that I was blind if I didn't see how you felt about me and I realized she was right. I was being willfully blind and stupid to ignore it. But I was afraid."

"We can deal with the fear together."

"Yeah."

He kissed her then, like he should have. It felt like something from a fairy tale, his hands on her hips, his mouth covering hers.

Chapter Nine

She'd been sautéing the garlic when her phone rang. Turning everything off, she'd left a note on her door and rushed to the hospital.

Kyle was in a state when she'd arrived, pacing and freaked out. Liv put her arms around his waist. "Hey there. I want you to focus, all right? She needs you to be calm just now."

"I can't. I'm trying but I keep thinking of worst case scenarios. What if something happens to her? To the baby?"

She kissed his cheek. "Everything is going to be all right, Kyle. Women do this every day. She's here in a hospital. She's healthy. The baby is healthy. She needs all of us to help. You don't have the luxury of shutting down and freaking out. She loves you and she needs you, so get your act together."

Polly came around the corner and Liv handed Kyle off to his mother and went in to Maggie. They'd just changed Maggie into a gown and hooked her up to a machine that echoed the baby's heartbeat through the room.

Relief showed clear on her face when she saw Liv.

"So, how's it goin?" Liv let the same fears Kyle had pass through her. She wasn't good at death, especially when it concerned the people she loved. Still, there was no time for fear in front of Maggie.

"I'm apparently having a kid and my husband is apparently having a nervous breakdown."

Liv moved a chair next to Maggie's bed.

"He loves you. None of this is in his control and he's freaked. He'll get it together. His mother is whipping him into shape now."

Maggie laughed and then winced. Liv reached out and took her hand, holding eye contact through the contraction.

"We've been through a lot you and me. We'll get through this too and at the end you'll be holding your precious baby son."

"You're the best. I'm so happy you and Marc finally found each other."

"I love him." Liv took a deep breath. "I finally admitted it to myself and I'm taking it from there. I'm scared all the time anyway, may as well be scared while I'm with him. Do you want to walk or use the ball? You tell me what you need."

"Good for you, Liv. I knew you were strong enough to handle this. I expect the whole damned Chase family has gathered out there. I can deal with visitors just now but I want to make it clear that I do not want an audience *or* cameras in here when the big moment comes. Pictures before, pictures after. No money shots."

Liv laughed. "Got it. No pictures of Maggie's hoo-ha with a baby emerging. I'll go let the hordes know you're available for visits."

Before too long, the room had filled with family and it had become a festive place. Whatever Polly told Kyle had calmed him but he didn't move more than an inch from Maggie's side.

They all took turns walking with Maggie through the halls as she labored.

On a break, Liv leaned into Marc, who massaged her shoulders. "Sorry about dinner, sport."

"I'll grab a rain check. This is more important. Have you eaten though? You want me to go and grab you something?"

"Not right now, but why don't you go and get something with Kyle? He needs a break and the nurse said Maggie has several more hours to go."

When the guys left, Liv turned down the lights and she, Cassie, Polly and Maggie all sat quietly. Maggie's pain had ramped up considerably and she finally opted for an epidural so she rested, staring at a television movie while Liv watched Cassie make jewelry.

It was right that they all sat in the room, the generations all together as a new life prepared to make an appearance. By the time the men returned with food for everyone but Maggie, who waved away any apologies for not being able to eat, Liv wanted to simply snuggle with Marc until the sun rose.

Who knew that love would make her so content? But it had. Content and the restlessness was gone. Everything felt like it was supposed to be. She'd never felt so settled and happy and she refused to entertain any of those, *oh no, what's going to happen to end this*, thoughts. Well, they were there in the background but she could beat them back.

Everyone but Liv and Kyle went to rest or nap in the waiting room when the labor nurse came to check on Maggie. She told them Maggie was just at four centimeters and they expected it to be several more hours before she'd be fully dilated.

Liv kissed Maggie's forehead. "You've got a ways to go. Rest for now. I'm going on a walk with Marc. I have my phone and I won't be far but you need to sleep. You won't if I'm here." She turned to Kyle. "Stretch out in that chair, it converts into a bed. You sleep too. She will if you will."

Kyle hugged Liv and she went out and found Marc waiting just outside the door.

"I need to walk, get some air. You want to come with me?"

"Of course. I wouldn't miss it." Marc took her hand as they went to inform the nurse's station that they'd be going on a walk for a while and to call if there was anything Maggie needed.

Once they'd gotten outside, Marc turned to her. "What do you need? You've been taking care of her all night, running interference, making sure no one pushed her too much."

She laid her head on his chest, listening to his heart. "I love you," she whispered, her voice trembling.

"Oh, sugar, I wanted to say it first. I love you too. I want this with you you know."

"You do?"

"I do what?"

She laughed. "You love me?"

"Woman, have you not listened to a damned thing I've said in the last months? Yes. Yes, I love you. It'd be impossible not to."

She smiled. "Oh. Good. And what is it you want with me?"

"So many ways I could go with that question. But being serious instead of lascivious for a moment at least, I want a family. A life like Kyle and Maggie, Shane and Cassie have."

"Marc, the age difference..."

"Stop it with that!" He pushed her back and shook his head. "That does not even matter. It's six years, not even quite six years. You act like it's twenty years. It seriously pisses me off."

"It pisses me off that you think it's nothing."

He wrinkled his nose. "Please. You're so full of shit for a woman who looks so good. I'm over twenty-one. And what difference could it make? Come on, sugar, it's six years. When you get old, I'll be old too. It's not like anyone is going to think I'm marrying you for your fortune because you're so old and hideous."

She laughed. "Stop that. I'm serious."

"So am I. Liv, tell me what difference our ages have to make in our relationship."

"You have time left to get out there and sow wild oats. I don't want you to settle down if you're not ready."

He snorted. "Olivia Jean Davis, girl, you are crazy. I've sowed 'em. Lots and lots of them. I don't have any more I want to sow except with you."

They walked a while longer as Liv let herself believe in what they had together and it grew inside her until it filled every cell. Almost every cell. The fear still crouched, small and nearly defeated. She could be loved by someone like this man, damn it. She would do it because he was worth it.

෨ഔഏരൃ

Liv walked out of Maggie's room, face bright with tears. "He's here. Nicholas Edward Chase is now ready to see two people at a time. Maggie is tired but she knows you all want to meet him. Polly, why don't you and Grandpa go first?"

Liv collapsed into a chair next to Marc and he hugged her. "You okay?"

"Oh my God. I've never in my life seen anything more amazing. Maggie deserves a medal. And Nicholas is the most beautiful boy. Looks an awful lot like your dad." She stood. "I need to call Dee and Penny. Maggie's dad is on his way here from the airport. I bet he's kicking himself for having to take a business trip when Maggie had the baby."

"Can I help with the calls?"

She smiled at him. "Thank you, darlin', but I need you to be the gatekeeper. You'll need to wrestle your parents out of there in about five minutes. Then Cassie and Shane can go in. Hopefully I'll be back but I need to go outside to call. Only two people and only five minutes. She needs to sleep. They all do."

She made her calls in the early afternoon heat. Smiling and crying as she relayed the details to Penny and Dee. Maggie would be so happy to see the flowers her students were going to send and Kyle's employees would take care of their accounts for the next two weeks so he could focus on Maggie and the baby.

It was then she saw Lindsay Cole walking out of the building across the street from the hospital. She looked up and flinched when she saw Liv. Liv expected to feel fury but she didn't. Instead she just felt sad that anyone could be so cold as Brody had been and Lindsay deserved him.

Liv had just been in the room to help her best friend deliver a new life into the world. No silly skank could ruin that. Not when she had Marc Chase in her bed and her heart.

She turned and went back inside.

Chapter Ten

Liv swayed in Marc's arms on the dance floor. The Honky Tonk on a Friday night and the place was packed. The Dixie Chicks played and Marc was lazily propositioning her in her ear. Shivers ran up and down her spine as he described in great detail just how he was going to make her come.

They'd foregone pool and beer at The Pumphouse and had gone on an actual date instead. Liv saw Shane and Cassie nearby and Matt sat with Amy Jackson at their table.

"What do you say?" Marc pulled away from her ear to look into her face.

"I'm not sure that's even physically possible but I'm up for it if you are."

He laughed and she felt light and dizzy with happy. Could have been the lack of sleep because Marc had slept over the last two nights and she'd been over at Kyle and Maggie's several times to check in. She wanted to bring by food but Polly had prepared enough food to keep them fed until Christmas.

"Okay. But a beer first to fortify me. Plus you realize this is our first actual out on the town date now that we're an official couple?"

"You mean all the times you came over to have sex didn't count?" Liv winked at him.

"Well, now yes they did. They did very fine. But this lets all these dimwits know you're mine. So no more sniffing around you every damned time you're out in public." He frowned as he led her off the dance floor.

"Me? You've got to be kidding. Marc, a stream of women follows you by scent. Everywhere you go there's some bimbo nearby fluttering her lashes and thrusting her boobies at you."

"Boobies?"

"Yes, that's how I think of them when their owner is twenty-two."

He blushed and it was her turn to laugh.

"Olivia Jean, are you jealous?"

"I don't like it, no."

He stopped right in the middle of the aisle they were walking on. "Do you think I'd do you like Brody?"

"No. No I don't. I wouldn't be with you if I did, Marc." She shrugged. "I didn't accuse you of cheating on me. You made a comment about men sniffing around and I countered with your harem. Every Chase brother comes equipped with one apparently. You asked if I was jealous and I answered you honestly. Don't ask a question if you don't want to hear the answer."

He relaxed and kissed her lightly. "I'm sorry. You're right. I just hate that you might compare me to Brody."

"I can understand that. But I wasn't. I don't like it that I have to wade through a bunch of women to get to you all the time."

"Doesn't signify. The only woman who matters is you." He took her hand and tucked it into his arm and continued to walk her to the table. When they got there, he pulled out her chair, enjoying the view as she plopped into it.

Lauren Dane

"Nice jiggle." He sat and poured her a beer from the pitcher.

"Hmpf. Hey, Matt."

"Hey Liv, how are you tonight? Looking mighty fine." Matt winked and Marc growled.

Matt just laughed. "It's payback for all you've done to Kyle and Shane."

"Just wait. You're the last one." Marc drank his beer while drawing circles on the back of Liv's neck with the other hand, loving the way she shivered in response. He noted the stares that Liv attracted but also the way she ignored it.

Until Brody came in with Lyndsay.

Everyone at the table froze except for Amy who waved and called out Lyndsay's name.

"No." Matt shook his head and put his hand on Amy's. "Neither of them is welcome at this table."

Amy looked confused and then her face changed when she caught sight of Liv, blushing. "I'm sorry. I didn't think."

Liv shrugged. "It's okay, Amy. I know you're friends with her."

"I know, but I wouldn't want her at my table either if I were you. Even though I think you got a way better deal." Amy smiled tentatively and Liv laughed.

"I know I did."

Lyndsay had been on her way over with Brody until she saw who else was at the table and froze. Brody saw Liv and paled. Marc narrowed his eyes at them both. He was thankful Brody's stupidity drove Liv to his arms but he hated the bastard for hurting her.

Shane and Cassie came up behind them and Marc noted with some amusement that Shane used a bit more of his body than was necessary to push past Brody. Cassie just stared at

144

them like she smelled something nasty. Brody and Lindsay moved to the other side of the dance floor.

"Asshole," Cassie muttered as she sat down.

Marc grinned as he looked around the table. His family was hers now too. He loved that she was so close to Cassie and Maggie. His family was important to him and she was already a part of it.

"It's a small town. We're bound to see each other. I'm surprised this is the first time I've seen him since the end of February." Liv took a sip of her beer.

"I'm sure he's been laying low. Everyone knows what he did. I told him what an ass I thought he was when I ran into him two months ago at the hardware store." Marc thought Brody should have been glad the running into him part wasn't with Marc's truck.

"You didn't tell me you ran into him." Liv raised an eyebrow at him in question.

Marc shrugged. "It didn't matter enough to mention. He's a punk and he's lucky I didn't put my fist in his face."

"Damn right," Cassie said.

"Marc and I are going to be getting out of here. He's got an ambitious new workout routine he's promised to show me."

Choking on his beer a moment, Marc stood with Liv and waved to everyone else as he dragged her out.

In the parking lot, he backed her against the side of his truck. "You're playing with fire, Liv." To underline his point, he rolled his hips, grinding his cock into her, inflamed even more when she half closed her eyes and moaned softly.

"You okay to drive?" Her hands skimmed over his shoulders and back as she writhed against him.

"I only had three sips of my beer before you dangled kinky sex in front of me. I'm as sober as a parson. If we don't get going right now, I'm going to do you right here in the parking lot."

"As tempting as that is, the family watching us through the window of the diner across the way might not appreciate it."

He stepped back and opened the door. She climbed up and in and he smiled, catching the flash of bare leg he got as she scooted across the seat to her side.

"My place is closer." He fastened his seatbelt quickly and put his keys in the ignition.

"Cool. I like having sex in your monument to bachelorhood."

"Where do you get the stuff you say?"

"I'm naturally gifted that way." She lifted her shoulders nonchalantly.

He drove safely but quickly to his apartment. Parking somewhat haphazardly, he dragged her up the stairs, pushed her inside and kicked the door closed behind him.

"Clothes off. Now."

She took a deep breath and undid the ties at the shoulder of her dress. It fell to the floor, pooling in a spill of deep blue at her feet.

"You had no panties on that whole time." He swallowed hard.

She shook her head. "Not a stitch."

"Damned sexy. And oh so naughty." He stalked toward her, yanking his shirt over his head, toeing his boots off when he reached her and tossing them back with the shirt.

"I have this recurring fantasy." He looked down at her, liking the way her mouth turned up at the corner when he said it.

"Oh? Do tell."

"It involves you, on your knees."

She dropped to her knees and he sucked in a breath.

"Like this?" She looked up at him.

"That'll do nicely. And then you suck my cock. Afterwards, we make love nice and slow. This after I go down on you of course."

She reached up and unzipped his jeans, freeing his cock. "Of course." Her tongue darted out to lick around the ridge of the head. Swirling her tongue around him as she took him farther and farther into her mouth. The heat built in him. Her mouth, hot and wet, surrounded him fully as her nails lightly scored his balls. Pleasure so intense he had to lock his knees to keep from crumbling, burst through him.

Liv thought she was pretty darned good at oral sex. Because she loved it. Loved making him squirm and groan, loved the feel of his cock in her mouth as it got harder and harder. There was power there, even on her knees, because it was her and no one else who made him feel that way.

Over and over again, she took him into her mouth, rocking back and sliding forward on him, keeping him wet and the pressure even. Every few passes she added a flick of her tongue just beneath the head.

His hands squeezed her shoulders, guiding her movements. No other man would have been allowed to do that but with him it seemed natural. Not overly aggressive or controlling in a negative sense but more like he couldn't resist because he needed her that much.

"You feel so good, sugar. I don't know what I did to deserve a gorgeous creature at my feet, sucking my cock, but I'm thankful to the powers that be for you. Fuck. Fuck. I'm close."

She hummed her approval around him and he cursed under his breath before he groaned low and long while he came.

He sank to the carpet beside her, bringing her to lie across his body as he caught his breath.

"Yeah. Better than the fantasy. Not that it'll stop me from having more fantasies about you or anything. Now I'll have more fodder."

She laughed and he rolled her over onto her back, looming over her. "That was spectacular, Liv. Now, I think it's your turn."

"Like I'm gonna argue?"

Marc looked down at her, lying there beneath him, naked but for some seriously sexy heels. The look in her eyes made his heart sing. Trust. Love. Openness.

The long line of her neck called to his lips and he didn't resist. Leaning in, he licked from shoulder to earlobe, loving the way she arched into him, giving him more of her neck.

No shy miss here. She widened her thighs and rolled her hips. Her fingers dug into his shoulders, urging him on.

Taking his time, he meandered over the hills and curves of her body, licking across her collarbone, laving his tongue through the warmth at the hollow of her throat. His fingers kneaded her muscles as he moved down, kissing the curve of her breast until he reached the nipple, swirling his tongue around it and sliding the edge of his teeth across it until she gasped.

"You like that?"

"Yes, oh yes. More, please, Marc."

"Since you asked so pretty." He continued to kiss down the bottom slope of her breast, over each rib, down the soft plane of her belly, pausing to dip his tongue in the sweet well of her navel.

Her low moan of encouragement made him grin as he sat back on his heels. Grabbing her ankles, he pushed her knees up and pressed them wide, opening her up to him completely.

She gasped and caught her bottom lip between her teeth.

"You need to keep your thighs wide for me. If you move them I'll stop. Can you do that for me, sugar?"

She blinked rapidly, licking her lips before managing a nod.

Satisfied, he slid his palms down her thighs and pulled her labia apart just before lowering his mouth to her and taking a leisurely lick. He felt her thigh muscles tense under his hands but she relaxed, keeping her legs open.

Sliding his tongue through her pussy, he reveled in the pleasure he brought her. He loved her taste, the way she responded so totally to him. The fingertip he'd had circling her gate slowly pushed into her and he closed his eyes against the way her body clasped around him.

A second finger followed the first and she arched her back. He paused and she moved her legs back in place.

"I find it quite erotic to control you, sugar. The way you just got even hotter and wetter says you do too."

She exhaled around a soft whimper and he got back to work, his tongue swirling and flicking around her clit over and over as he fucked into her with his fingers.

Her clit bloomed against his tongue as she cried out softly, her thighs wrapping around his shoulders as she came.

Finally she went lax, her thighs falling open and he put his head on her belly, looking up the line of her body at her face, a relaxed smile on her lips.

He kissed her belly and stood, holding a hand out to her. She took it and he helped her up.

"Condoms in my bathroom. Just bought a new box today. You keep me very busy." He pulled her down his hallway but she stopped at the doorway when he went inside.

He saw her reflection in the mirrors over the sink, saw the mirrored doors on the closet and realized the entire room was walled by mirrors. He smiled. "Come on in here." He patted the counter. "I think this is the perfect height."

Shucking his jeans and socks, he hoisted her up on the counter, stepping between her thighs and going in for a kiss.

"I like this view. I can see your ass and the muscles in your back. You have a very sexy behind."

"Why thank you, ma'am. I do try." He winked, sheathing himself quickly and testing her for readiness before slowly pushing himself into her.

Liv watched him make love to her from every angle, really appreciating the mirrors on the closet door fully. Watched the clutch of his glutes as he pushed his cock into her, the flex of his shoulders and down the long line of his back.

She caught sight of her body wrapped around his, the paler skin of her legs contrasted with the more golden hues of his. Her eyes, slumberous, lips parted. They were beautiful together, linked.

It was almost as if she watched someone else there in the mirror. Perhaps through his eyes? In the mirror she was confident and trusted him completely as he stoked her desire that he'd just sated scant minutes before.

His body was made to fit into hers and he did it so very well. His cock, wide with a blunt head, brushed over her sweet spot over and over. He knew just where it was and took great care to give it attention. That's how their sex was. Mindblowing yes, but because he *wanted* it to be. For her.

"I like seeing you from all these angles. So pretty." A fingertip traced around her nipples, feather light. "These are luscious. When I see you my mouth waters to taste them."

His head bent then, the warmth of his tongue sent shivers up her spine as he flicked over the nipple quickly, in time with his thrusts.

How he did it she didn't know but it was a form of erotic torture and he devastated her with it time and again. Each flick was followed by a sucking pull that brought a throb from her clit.

"I love the way your pussy flutters around me when I do that. Such sensitive nipples."

"For you."

He looked into her eyes then, pausing. "I love you, Liv."

She felt it to her toes and blinked back tears. "I love you too."

His free hand found her clit, squeezing it lightly between slippery fingers and she arched, grinding herself into him, into his thrusts as yet again, climax washed through her body, leaving her helpless to do much more than hold on and ride it out.

"There you go, sugar. Give it to me," he said, voice hoarse as his thrusts deepened once, twice and a third time before he pressed as deep as he could and came.

And as if she weighed nothing, he picked her up and carried her to his bed, laying her there carefully, gently.

"Rest up now because we're going another round or five when I get my breath back."

Laughing, she reached up and traced the line of his jaw. "Even if my legs were working I wouldn't want to escape."

Chapter Eleven

Liv stood under the tree the large blankets were spread beneath for the annual homecoming picnic. Nicholas, two months old now, stared up at her, wide eyed with a gummy grin on his face.

"Aren't you just the most handsome little man?" Liv smooched his chubby cheeks and smoothed down the patch of bright red hair that normally stood straight up on the top of his otherwise bald head.

"Handsome? Well, certainly he's got a lot of character but with that hair, I don't know." Matt grabbed a bare foot and kissed it, making Nicholas emit a breathy laugh.

"A man with character is handsome, I'll have you know." Polly stood there, moving from foot to foot and Liv finally took pity on her and handed the baby over.

"You're greedy with him." Polly never took her eyes from Nicholas as she teased Liv. "You should have one of your own and you can hold him. Well, every once in a while because he'll fit just fine here on my other hip."

Marc laughed, a little distracted. He'd run into one of his old ex-girlfriends the day before and she she'd come on to him. Strong. It wasn't so much that he was interested but there'd been a moment when part of him panicked at the thought of never being with another woman again. It passed quickly enough as he'd realized he didn't want to be with another woman. Liv was everything.

He'd considered talking to her about it but he'd been concerned that he'd hurt her or make her think he was having second thoughts. He'd worked so hard and so long to gain her trust, he didn't want to endanger that. But he felt like he was hiding something from her because they normally shared everything.

"You okay?" Her head cocked, hand on her hip, she looked so beautiful it made his chest hurt a moment.

"Yeah, fine. Hungry? We've got a lot of food here and I can see Momma has left us all to fend for ourselves now that the youngest Chase has stolen her attention."

Liv sat next to him on the blanket and began to make plates and pass them down to everyone. Cassie sat across from them, leaning against Shane while Maggie looked up at Polly as Polly sang silly songs to the baby. It was good there with the people he loved.

Since Nicholas's birth, he and Liv had gotten closer and closer. He practically lived in her house and saw her or spoke to her daily. She'd become a regular at all Chase family events and dinners.

He loved waking up to her, feeling the warmth of her body next to his. They'd cooked together, side by side and he'd enjoyed the feeling of familiarity and comfort. Their sex life had remained active, exciting and very frequent. But it wasn't just sex, every time he was inside her he learned something new about her and himself. She saw into him. There was a time he'd have been freaked out by that, but instead, it made him feel whole.

He didn't want to do anything to screw that up and so he'd keep the thing with Nancy to himself because it had meant nothing anyway.

Liv knew there was something Marc wasn't telling her. She'd known him long enough to tell the difference between the way he was acting then and his normal behavior.

She didn't like it. It felt familiar. Before the end with her other lovers it had been like this. Smiles and assurances that nothing was wrong and then the end. Her insecurity ramped up.

All afternoon and into the evening it sat at the back of her mind, worrying her, nagging at her. Finally, as they were packing Nicholas and all his gear into Maggie's car, her friend turned to her, touching her cheek.

"Is everything all right? I feel like I've not paid a lot of attention to you these last two months. Nicholas takes up so much of my time but I want to know what's going on with you. I care about you."

Liv gave Maggie a tight smile. "I'm fine. I think. I don't know." She sighed. "It's Marc. Since yesterday afternoon when I came into the shop to work out he's been acting odd. I don't know, like he's not saying something."

"Are you two having problems?"

"No. Things have been going great. He's totally present in this relationship, you know? We talk all the time, share everything. I've never felt this way before. He's good to me, you know? He cares about me. But I'm afraid." A sob tore from her and Maggie hugged her.

"It's okay. He loves you. He does. I've seen the way he looks at you. I've heard how he talks about you. I'm sure it's stress or something silly like that."

"I'm afraid he's going to leave me." Liv felt like the words tore a part of her to say. Like everyone she loved left. Sooner or later it happened.

"Oh honey, don't cry. I'd give everything I own to bet on Marc loving you. Just give it some time. I'm sure he'll relax and all this will seem silly in a few days."

Kyle approached with Marc and Shane, all holding stuff to load into the cars and Liv quickly dried her eyes and stood back.

"Call me tomorrow, okay?"

Liv nodded. She leaned down to kiss Nicholas' head as he slept in his carseat. "Night, sweetie."

Kyle looked at her, a question in his eyes but she shook her head and he moved his gaze to Maggie who shrugged.

"Everything okay?" Marc asked as he took Liv's hand.

"You tell me."

"Okay, what the hell is going on?" Kyle asked.

"Nothing, hon. Liv, you call me tomorrow, you hear? Marc, goodnight and make sure you take care of our girl." Maggie gave him a stern look and got into the car.

"Liv, honey, have you been crying?" Marc touched her face gently.

"It doesn't matter. I want to go home."

He helped her into his truck and drove back to her place.

"It does matter." He turned to her once he'd pulled into her driveway. "Tell me what's wrong."

"You're the one who's not telling me what's wrong, Marc. I can tell there's something up but you won't say and that makes me wonder just what it is you're hiding."

"Sugar, I'm not hiding anything. I love you. You believe that, don't you?"

"I want to."

Marc's heart began to pound at the desolate sound of that answer. God, he'd made her so upset without even trying to and now if he told her it would make it even worse. She'd think he was hiding it because it meant something instead of just a stupid thing that he didn't say anything about and now had snowballed.

He moved over to her side and pulled her to him, holding her tight. "I love you, Olivia. More than anything. I swear that on my life. I'm just stressed, honey. It has nothing to do with how I feel about you."

Nodding against his chest she hugged him back. "I need you to tell me stuff, okay? I can't bear thinking that you're having second thoughts or something and not telling me."

He tipped her chin up, kissing her lips. "I love you. I don't doubt that for a moment. Now let's go inside, okay?"

ജോയോൽ

Things had gotten back to normal pretty much and Liv relaxed. Maggie had been relieved that everything was all right and Liv realized that things were going the best they had her entire life. Her plan had actually come to fruition and loving Marc Chase had been everything she'd imagined true love to be and more.

A spring in her step, she walked toward the studio a bit early on a Wednesday. The heat had finally edged away and fall was in the air. She'd picked up a few brochures for a bed and breakfast down on the coast. She thought a nice weekend away would be just the thing for them.

Pushing open the front door of the studio, Liv halted. The smile on her face froze and then slid off as a pain so sharp she wasn't sure she'd survive it sliced through her gut.

Marc was there on the floor, on top of another woman, Nancy Ellis. Nancy's thighs were spread and wrapped around him.

Nancy, laughing looked up and caught sight of Liv as Marc pushed away and scrambled up. When he turned and saw her he went as pale as a ghost.

"Sugar, it's..."

"Not what I think?" She felt totally empty, as if there was nothing inside her at all, which she supposed was better than the searing pain she'd felt just before.

"You made me think I was imaging things." She took a step back and he took one forward. "Don't. Don't you fucking come near me. Not ever again. Don't call me. Don't come see me." She pressed a fist to her gut to keep from screaming as the pain came back, filling her from her toes up to her ears. She would not cry. She would not give him the satisfaction.

Turning, she left and he was on her heels.

"Liv, damn it, wait!" He grabbed her arm and she spun, kneeing him square in the balls, smiling with savage satisfaction as he crumpled to his knees.

"Don't you touch me. You fucking bastard." Turning again she ran as fast as she could.

Knowing he'd probably go to her place, she grabbed her car and got the hell out of there.

𝈪𝈫𝈬𝈭

Marc had been busy with one of his clients when he'd turned to see Nancy walk in. *Great.*

"Hey, Nancy. What brings you here?"

She put her hand on her hip and gave him her sexiest smile. "I came for a workout."

His other client had been cooling down and by the time she'd gone, it was just Marc and Nancy.

"Well, I told you that I'm with Liv Davis and I meant that. If you'd like to work out without any sex involved, I'd be happy to help. I'm not taking one-on-one clients just now but I have a wait list. But you can use the facilities here without a personal trainer."

She'd appeared to take the news well and had gone back to change and he'd filled out enrollment papers and gotten her signed up. He should have known it was too good to be true when she'd said she was having trouble with one of the machines. He'd bent over her to help and she'd pulled him down, laughing, wrapping her thighs around his waist.

Pissed off beyond measure, he pushed himself away from Nancy and to standing when he'd heard a gasp. A sound that constricted around his heart. He'd turned, knowing she was there but that knowledge hadn't been enough to prepare him for the look on her face.

Her voice, flat, empty didn't fit with the pain glittering in her eyes. He had plenty of time to relive the entire event as he lay there on the sidewalk after his gloriously pissed off woman had kneed him in the balls and took off running.

He limped back into the studio where Nancy stood, fully dressed and looking upset.

"Oh goodness, Marc. I didn't... I'm so sorry. Is she all right?"

"I don't know," he said, voice strained as his balls throbbed. "What the hell were you thinking?"

"I was just flirting. I didn't mean for that to happen. I may have wanted you back and wanted to test to see what your commitment to Liv really was, but I'd never, not ever in a million years want to hurt her like that. Or you. I'm so sorry." Nancy wrung her hands anxiously. "Do you want me to talk to her? Tell her what happened?"

"Not for now. Maybe later. Fuck." He pushed a hand through his hair. "I have to go find her." He put up the closed sign and Nancy left, promising to be available to talk to Liv if he needed her to.

ഇരുന്ന

Maggie opened her front door and her warm greeting died in her throat. She reached out and pulled Liv inside.

"My goodness, honey, what is it? Is everyone okay? Who got hurt?"

"Marc," she gasped.

"Marc got hurt? What happened? Where is he?" Kyle came into the room.

"Marc cheated on me." Liv crumpled to her knees as she wept as if her heart would break.

"He what? No. No, he wouldn't!" Maggie sank to scoop Liv into her arms and rock her slowly. "Honey, you must have misunderstood."

"Two weeks ago he was h-hiding something and tonight I found him on the floor with Nancy Ellis. He was on top of her, her legs wrapped around him. She was l-laughing."

"This can't be right. Liv, honey, my brother adores you. He would not do this to you. I know it." Kyle looked helplessly at Liv as he brushed a hand over her hair. "Did he explain?"

"Explain what? Do you think I'm a moron? Or some desperate woman who'll buy a bunch of lies to hold onto a bigger lie?"

"Let's get you up and on the couch, all right? Kyle's gonna go and make us some tea and we're going to talk after you finish your cry." Maggie raised a brow at Kyle who left the room quickly.

"I love him so much. My God this hurts more than anything I've ever felt before. This is not right. Why would he do this? If he wasn't ready he shouldn't have pushed me. I was...I had a plan! Damn it, I had a plan and he promised he loved me and I fell in love with him and he sucks. Oh he sucks and I hate him and I hope I did permanent damage when I kneed him in the sac. That fucker."

Maggie sighed heavily, not knowing what to do but hoping like hell Kyle picked up her hint and was tracking down his brother to find out what was happening.

"I tell you something, Olivia Jean, if Marc has cheated on you, I will personally skin him alive. I swear it. I've got your back. But let's not be hasty here. Let him explain."

"Explain what? Maggie, he was on top of another woman with her legs wrapped around his waist! What is there to explain about that that isn't totally obvious?"

"Okay so it sounds pretty bad." And boy how it did. What the hell did Marc do? "But..."

Liv stood. "No buts, Maggie. I never should have allowed myself to get close to him. I should have listened to my head and not my freaking vagina. I have been such a fool. This probably isn't even the first time."

Kyle came into the room and put a tray down on the table with a pot of tea and some mugs. "I'm going to go check on the baby. Should I make up the guest room for you, sweetie?"

"No. No. I need to go. Be alone. I have to think."

"I don't think that's a good idea. You should be with people who love you right now. Stay here, please. You know Nicholas adores his auntie. Stay here tonight and we'll have pancakes tomorrow morning."

"Oh, I'm having biscuits and gravy and six slices of bacon tomorrow morning. Maybe a cheeseburger for lunch. But I don't want to be around Nicky in this mood, it's not good for him to see me this way. I'm sorry, I shouldn't have come."

"Of course you should. Liv, you're my best friend. You've been there for me when I've needed you for thirty years. Please, let me be there now." Maggie took her hands, aching at the pain on Liv's face.

Liv kissed Maggie's cheek. "I love you for being my friend, I truly do. But I know Kyle called Marc when he was in the kitchen and I don't want to see his face. I can't." She moved to the door. "I'll call you when I'm ready."

She turned and left and Maggie stared at the door with tears in her eyes.

"He's on his way but he was at her house when I called so he won't make it. Let me call him back."

Maggie turned to her husband. "And tell him what? She didn't tell me where she was going because she didn't trust me not to tell Marc. Kyle, I've betrayed her today just like your dumbass brother did."

Kyle took her in his arms. "You didn't betray her. You wanted to help her and make this thing right. He says it was all a stupid misunderstanding. That she walked in at the wrong moment."

"Clearly! I'm sure he was hoping to finish up by the time his *girlfriend* walked in on him between another woman's legs."

"That isn't what it was. Or it is but not what it looked like. Maggie, damn it, I love Liv. I would not cheat on her." Marc walked into the room. "Where is she?"

"Gone. I don't know where. But you'd better have a damned good explanation."

Marc sighed and sat down heavily on the couch, telling them everything.

ಬಂಬಂಜಿ

"Do you know where she is?" Polly asked, pacing.

"She left a voicemail for Cassie saying she didn't want her to be put in the middle between her friends and her family but she was okay and would be gone for a while," Shane said. "Cassie's all torn up over it. She's upset that Liv is alone right now and didn't think she could turn to her or Maggie."

"I could just knock the spit out of that Nancy," Maggie said, patting Nicholas's back.

"If I could just get her to talk to me, I know I could get her to see some sense," Marc said heavily. "I've left her messages and notes at her house. She's not gone back there since Wednesday night. They told Maggie, Liv took a week's vacation from work. No one is talking to me. I wouldn't cheat on her, I swear it. I know it looks bad but I'm not that man. Not now and I wasn't even a cheater before I fell for my girl. God, I hate thinking about her out there believing I'd betray her like that. I just want to hold her and love her."

Polly squeezed his shoulder and kissed his cheek. "Honey, this will be all right. We've got to find her and let her know she's loved by all of us."

€ƒ

In Atlanta, Liv sat, eyes closed, relaxation a lá white wine and a facial.

"Just relax here for a while longer. The deep cleansing mask will be done in about ten minutes and your hands will be ready to come out of the paraffin," the disembodied voice of the beautician told her.

"Mmmm. Thanks," Liv mumbled, settling deeper into the chair.

"Oh girl, you're a sneaky one."

Liv sighed, knowing it was too good to be true that she'd remained unmolested for the last week.

"What are you doing here? Where's Nicholas?"

"What the hell is on your face? Nicholas is right here in my arms if you'd opened your eyes to see."

"What are you doing here?"

"You already asked that and your eyes are closed still. Don't you want to see your godson? He's missed you, you know. Gone for a week without a damned word. I mean really. I ought to sic Polly on you."

Liv cracked an eye and turned her head. "Hi, lumpkin, how are you, sweetie?" Nicholas cooed at her and reached toward her voice. "In a few minutes, bubba. Right now Auntie Liv's hands are wrapped in wax. I know, silly, aren't I?"

"Not as silly as having that green crap on your face."

"Deep cleansing mask with milk and chamomile. Are we here to trade beauty tips?"

"Lookit you with that smart mouth."

"Look, Maggie, what do you want?"

Just then the beautician came back to clean off her mask, put on some moisturizer, remove the wax from her hands and massage them.

"I'll skip the manicure today, Sarah. My godson here is sensitive to smells."

Liv paid her bill and left a tip, not looking at Maggie as she went toward the doors.

"You are so not going to just walk out on me, Olivia Davis. Thanks to Dee and Penny, I tracked you down. We've all been worried as hell about you. How dare you not keep in contact?"

Liv spun and glared at her oldest friend. "I would say something very unladylike right now but Nicholas is watching so I'll just tell you to mind your own beeswax. I've been looking at apartments here. I've gone on two job interviews. I'm moving on thankyouverymuch. I haven't kept contact because you have other allegiances now as does Cassie. I thought I could trust Dee and Penny but I guess I was wrong. Give me that baby."

Maggie handed Nicholas over who giggled and reached up to touch her face. "Hey, lumpkin." She kissed his tiny face, missing the way he smelled.

"What the heck does that mean? Other allegiances?"

"You know what it means. Where's Marc? Hiding somewhere ready to jump out? With his new girlfriend at his place?"

Maggie sighed. "Okay, this is what we're going to do. You're not going to take this attitude with me. Other allegiances my ahh—booty." Maggie looked at Nicholas. "Then you and I are going to your hotel and we're going to put the baby down for a nap. You're going to tell me about this fool plan to move away from Petal and I'm going to knock you out if you go through with it. And then we're going to order room service and talk about Marc over a few beers."

"Do I have any choice?"

"My next step is to call Polly Chase. She's more agitated than I am over this so she'll drive out here like a shot. You decide." Maggie folded her arms over her chest.

"Straight to first strike nuclear war." Liv shook her head. "You've gotten vicious in your old age."

"Exactly. What'll it be?"

Sighing, Liv handed Nicholas back to his mother. "Fine. I'm sure you know what room I'm in."

Stalking off, Liv headed for her car and the hotel. When she arrived, she waited for Maggie in the lobby.

Maggie looked surprised when she saw Liv waiting. "What's the problem?"

"I figured you'd have a bunch of baby gear and would need help carrying it."

"Tough guy. Total marshmallow in the center." Maggie smiled and handed Nicholas to her along with his baby bag. "Take him on up with you, I'm going back to the car to get his porta-crib."

"Come on you, you're the best man I've taken to a hotel room ever." Liv kissed his forehead and took him upstairs.

She'd changed a diaper and was singing him some Aretha Franklin when Maggie knocked on the door and moved to set up his crib.

"I'm going to nurse him down. Order me something good to eat and settle in. We have a lot to talk about and I'm staying over."

"Bossy."

"Damned right. Get to it, I'm hungry."

Twenty minutes later, Nicholas was sleeping in the bedroom and the food arrived. Liv cracked open a beer and sat back, looking at Maggie. "So? Go on, tell me."

"You tell me. What kind of stupid shit is this? Moving to Atlanta? Why? Over a stupid misunderstanding with your boyfriend? Even if he had cheated on you, which he didn't, why would a woman like Liv Davis let anyone chase her out of her own damned town?"

"Because that woman can't keep a damned man, Maggie. I don't want to be her anymore. I don't want to be there anymore. I'm making a clean break and starting over here. A new city and a new outlook. I'll find the right man here and I won't have to see Marc Chase's face ever again."

"He loves you, damn it. What you saw was Nancy acting a fool. I talked with the stupid cow a few days ago. She faked a problem with her machine and when he leaned in to help her she grabbed him with her legs. He'd just pushed away from her when you walked in. He was ready to rip a hank off her hide. He's sorry you're hurt. He knows it looked bad but it only *looked* bad. Honey, he loves you. He's been miserable since you've been gone."

"Oh boo hoo. What about me, huh? I couldn't even go to my best friend without her calling Marc. I couldn't talk to my other best friend because she's married to that fink's other brother. My best guy friend is his other damned brother. And I'm in a hotel an hour and a half away and my other two friends finked me out as well. Why does Marc get all the consideration here?"

"I'm sorry! Liv, honey, I am truly sorry I hurt you. I just wanted to help. I know he loves you. I know you love him. I didn't mean to drive you away." Maggie took her hand and squeezed it. "Of all the people in my life, you've been there for me the longest. When no one else loved me, you did. When no one else cared about how I was feeling or how I did on an exam, you did. When no one else remembered my birthday, you did. It breaks my heart that you feel you can't count on me. Please forgive me. Honestly, I can't bear it that you feel you can't trust me."

Liv sighed. "I understand why you did it. I just needed to be alone. I needed to think."

"Well you haven't been thinking at all if you think moving away is a logical way to deal with this. Do you think Marc is just going to let you walk away? Liv, haven't you heard anything I've said about that night?"

"I have. I heard it from him too via voicemails."

"And?"

"And I don't know. I've been thinking about it and wondering if I believed him but really I suppose the problem is that I have to think about it to begin with."

"What does that mean?"

"I mean if I really trusted him and if he was truly trustworthy, would I have had to think on it for a week? Would I doubt him at all?"

"Liv, you know, I can't do this for you. I can tell you my opinion, which is that Marc is telling the truth. That he loves you. That he's worth trusting. I can also tell you that you love him. But there's something else inside you that you never quite share with me. Doesn't mean I can't see it though. Fear that you're not good enough."

Liv shrugged, feeling the shame of it roil in her gut.

"You act so tough. So in charge and confident but there's something always in the back of your mind, isn't there? Telling you that you don't deserve forever. So you're going to jump on something like this to keep from taking a big step with a man who is your match. And he is, Liv. These other men, Brody, Matt, you've enjoyed them and had long term things with them but they weren't your equal. Not the way Marc is. You can't manage him or keep him walled out and that scares you."

Liv chewed her bottom lip, blinking fast to hold back tears. "I want forever. I do."

"I know you do. And you *deserve* it too. But in order to have it, you have to risk your heart and really trust yourself as much as you need to trust Marc. Trust that you deserve to be loved. I had to risk that, risk my heart and take the leap when Kyle came along. I was scared shitless but hell, look at us now. A mortgage, a kid, a mother-in-law who fills my house with so much baby gear I can barely walk. I figure if you marry Marc, she'll spend some of her energy on you and I'll get a break."

"I don't know if I can. If I take him back and he cheats, I don't know if I can survive it. When I saw him there with Nancy like that...I've never in my life felt that kind of pain. Not even when I lost my mother did it feel so awful, so hopeless. I don't want to experience that again." Liv toyed with the food on her plate but didn't eat anything.

"Up until the homecoming picnic, I've never seen you happier. It felt good didn't it? Right?"

Liv thought about it. Had been thinking about it for the last week. "Yes. Yes it did. I felt whole for the first time in my life. But that changed at the picnic because then I began to panic that there was something wrong and he'd dump me any day. I hate feeling like that. It was that way with Matt, just waiting for the other shoe to drop. I want to feel safe. Secure in my relationship. I don't think it's too much to ask."

Maggie nodded. "It isn't too much to ask. Why don't you talk to Marc about all this? See what he says?"

"Because he lied to me, Maggie."

"I told you, he didn't cheat on you."

Liv held up a hand to cut her off. "I know that. I'm pretty sure of it anyway. It was a public place. Plus if he had and I'd busted him, he'd have stopped trying to lie about it after a few days and moved on to another woman."

"Then what are you talking about?"

"The homecoming picnic. There was something wrong and not something about his work. I don't know what exactly it was, but I know he lied about it and I let it go. I let it go because I was afraid and I know now I can't live that way."

"Give him a chance to explain, Liv. He's fallen apart this week without you. You have nothing left to lose. You're already in love with him. Don't run away from the best thing that's ever happened to you. I want you to be happy. You *are* happy with Marc. Don't let fear take this chance at a future with the man you love away from you."

Nicholas woke up then with a cry and Maggie went to get him.

"Does Marc know you're here?" Liv asked as settled back in to feed the baby.

"He does. He was so worried I wanted to let him know you were safe and that I was coming to see you. He agreed not to come and bother you until I'd spoken to you. Well, after Polly interceded and talked him out of rushing out here to grab you by the hair and drag you home."

Liv laughed. "Yeah, he does have that caveman thing going on. Surprising really. I'd never have suspected it. He always seemed the laid back skirt chaser. But he's got an iron spine beneath that exterior."

"He's never had to fight for anything he wanted and stood to lose before." Maggie shrugged. "I need to call Kyle and let him know I got here okay. I just texted him when we got here earlier. He was uneasy to have me come to stay the night with Nicholas away from him."

"Go home, Mags. You'll be back in Petal by nine and everyone will feel better. Your husband wants you in his bed tonight and he wants to know that his baby is okay. That's his right and you want that too. I'm not running off again. In fact I'll be back in town by Sunday."

"Really? It's no big deal to stay here. I'm not far away. He knows I'm all right and I want to be here when you need me. I'm still pissed that you ran off."

"Honey, Nicholas is a precious little bundle of fabulous. Take that lumpkin home to his daddy. And tough. I did it for myself."

"You'll talk to Marc?"

"Probably. I don't know."

"But you'll be back by Sunday for sure, you promise?"

Liv held up her pinky. "Pinky swear."

She helped load them into the car and waved them on their way back home.

Chapter Twelve

On her way back from a small shopping trip, Liv stopped at the cemetery near the hospital. Heading to the back corner near the large oak tree, she walked from the car to the headstone.

Laying lilacs down on the marker she knelt, brushing the dust off the letters that made up her mother's name.

"I have the urge to lay down and start singing a Madonna song, Mom." Liv laughed to herself.

"So there's this guy. Okay, *the* guy. I love him so much it's not funny. This is the same one I told you about the last time I was here and yeah, the time before."

Liv traced a finger over the purple explosion of flowers as she spoke, relating the whole story to herself, wishing her mom really had been there to hear the whole thing and give her advice.

People you loved left you. They died. They moved to Florida. They married and had kids. Things changed and change was scary. If you kept a part of yourself back, protected, it never got hurt. Did it?

Sighing, she arranged the flowers her sister had most likely left and arranged her own with them before standing. Brushing her pant legs off, she walked back to her car, wondering what the price of that little bit of safety was and whether it was worth it.

Head down, bearing packages, she walked down the hall to her hotel room, thinking about all that had happened.

"Let me help you with your burdens."

The caramel drawl made her stop in her tracks and look up. Marc stood in front of her door.

Her eyes took a lazy tour from the toes of his battered cowboy boots, up the faded denim covering the powerful legs, the deep blue sweater she'd given him on a whim, the face, the handsome set of the jaw, those gorgeous green eyes and the tousled hair. Beautiful. The man was flat out beautiful.

He held out a hand and gently tugged on the bags she held and she let go, letting him take them while she unlocked the door and held it open for him.

He put them down and turned to face her, saying nothing but his gaze took her in hungrily.

"Oh, sugar." He reached out and traced the curve of her bottom lip with the pad of his thumb. "I've missed you. And here you are with an ache in your eyes that tears at my heart. Will you talk to me?"

"Marc..."

"Olivia Jean Davis, I love you. Damn it, please. Are you going to make me beg? I will. But I'd prefer to ask you and have you agree to talk to me, hear me out."

"Sit." She waved at a chair. "I need to put the bags in the bedroom. I'll be back in a minute."

Marc waited until she'd left the room before heaving a relieved sigh. She looked tired and thin and he wanted nothing more than to scoop her into his arms and take care of her. He doubted she'd let him at that point though.

Instead he grabbed the room service menu and flipped through it. Cobbling together an order, he called down and arranged to have it brought up.

She may have looked tired and thin but she was still the most beautiful thing he'd ever seen. She was there and he was there, at least he'd gotten that far.

Maggie had called to say she wasn't staying over in Atlanta with Liv and Marc had gone over to their house to wait for her to get an update. She didn't tell him a lot and he knew that part of it was that she didn't want Liv to feel betrayed. But she did tell him she thought he still had a chance to make things right between them.

He could have waited for her to come back by Sunday like she'd told Maggie she was planning to. But he didn't want to. He wanted to go to her and lay it all out. They'd hammer things out once and for all and leave together on Sunday morning or he'd leave alone. Okay, he'd leave alone and then work to get her back after trying to convince himself he didn't need her for a few weeks. But they had to work it out, the last walls had to come down between both of them or they'd never be able to move forward.

She came out a few minutes later, having changed into the soft yoga pants she thought he hated. In truth, they made her look even sexier with the way they lovingly hugged her ass and long legs.

Gracefully, she folded herself into the matching chair across from his. "Are you hungry? I haven't eaten since breakfast. We could order up some food if you'd like."

"Did you even eat breakfast? Liv, sugar you look like you haven't been eating much at all."

She shrugged. He didn't like the dull look in her eyes.

"I took the liberty of ordering us up some dinner and a bottle of wine while you were in the other room. It should be here in a few minutes."

"I'm going to order some chocolate cheesecake. I've been having a slice or two every day." She moved to grab the phone.

"I already did."

"You did? It's got like eight thousand calories in it."

He laughed. "Oh I see. You're trying to agitate me, is that it? Well too late, I'm already agitated. You haven't been taking care of yourself. That agitates me. A slice of cheesecake isn't going to kill you. And if you've been eating it daily, it doesn't show."

Snorting, she rolled her eyes.

"I didn't cheat on you."

"I know."

He jerked his head back, surprised. "You know?"

She shrugged.

"What the fuck is that shrug? If you knew I didn't cheat on you why the hell did you bolt?"

"If I want to shrug, I'll shrug. Don't you tell me not to shrug. I'll shrug if I want to." Her chin stuck out defiantly and he fought the ridiculous urge to grin at her. "And I didn't decide to believe that you hadn't cheated until yesterday."

He moved toward her but she put a hand out to stay him. "What? If you know I didn't cheat on you, why aren't we making up right this moment?"

"Because that's not everything and if you don't know that, we're worse off than I imagined."

Room service arrived and set up while she looked out the window. He signed the receipt, tipped the guy and put out the *Do Not Disturb* sign before closing and locking the door.

He moved to stand behind her, lightly resting his hands on her hips, relieved when she let him. "Liv," he laid his head on her shoulder, "I love you. It's killing me that there's this wall between us. Let me in."

"Do you know who first called me Liv?"

He took the opportunity to wrap his arms around her waist and pull her closer. "No. Maggie?"

"My mom. She was Olivia too, you know?"

"I remember that. I don't remember much else about her though."

"My dad, he loved her so much it was like my sister and I barely existed if she was in the room. Anyway, she started calling me Liv to give me something separate from her name, to set us apart a bit."

"How old were you when she died?"

"Thirteen. She got sick when I was eight."

"I'm sorry. It's got to be hard. I can't imagine."

"It was. Anyway, she told me once that her favorite thing about my father was her ability to trust him totally. That she could rely on him no matter what."

Ah, there it was. He'd been wondering why she'd chosen that moment to share that story about her mother.

"Nancy faked a problem with one of the machines and when I..."

"Yes, yes, I know." She moved away and he felt her absence acutely. "I told you, I believe you didn't cheat on me. Believe me, Marc, if I thought you fucked Nancy you'd be coughing up blood right now. Whether or not she'll find herself in that situation if I catch her ass in town is another thing."

"I'm lost, sugar."

"No you're not. And this is seriously pissing me off."

"What the hell are you talking about, Liv? If you know I didn't cheat on you, why are you pissed off?"

"Because I can't trust you, that's why. And you need to get the hell out of here right now if you're going to play stupid."

"You're going to sit and eat and we're going to talk right now." Clenching his jaw, he stalked back to the table and began to uncover dishes.

"You need to cut that bossy shit out right now." She sat and put a napkin on her lap.

"Shut up and eat."

She narrowed one eye at him and he felt better at seeing her spark back, even if it was directed at him.

"I could just say I'm sorry to end this argument but I'd rather know what I'm sorry for."

"You. Lied. To. Me." She took a rather vicious bite of her fish and washed it down with a sip of red wine.

"When did I lie to you?"

The growl she emitted would have been cute if her eyes hadn't looked so dangerously angry.

"On the night of the homecoming picnic. There was something wrong. I *know* there was and I know it wasn't about your stress level like you said. I know it was about me. But I let it go and I shouldn't have. I was a coward because I didn't want to rock the boat and lose you. But the doubts were worse than losing you. You lied to me, Marc."

He sat back, wiping his lips.

"I did. But it wasn't important and it only would have upset you."

"Please go. When I come back to Petal, just leave me alone. It'll be easier if we make a clean break."

"Whoa!" He put his hands up. "What the hell? I'm not leaving and I'm sure as hell not making a clean break. I told you it wasn't important. It wasn't."

"We'll make one if I say so." Her jaw clenched and panic ate at his insides.

"What is it you want, Liv? Tell me and I'll give it to you. I love you, damn it."

"I want your *honesty*, Marc. We're supposed to be partners and you're hiding things. Lying to me and when you're busted you have the audacity to sit there and tell me it was for my own good? It wasn't important enough for you to tell me the truth? Is that what I'd have to look forward to as your girlfriend? Honesty when you decide it's important?"

Oh crap. He was in a corner and it was of his own making.

"The day before the picnic, I bumped into Nancy in town. She came on to me pretty strong. There was a moment, just a moment, when I panicked. Felt a bit smothered and had a bit of a, *man I'm only going to be with one woman for the rest of my life*, moment. But it passed in a few minutes and I realized I didn't want to be with anyone else but you for the rest of my life."

She jammed a piece of bread into her mouth, clearly angry. She watched him as she finished off her glass of wine and got herself another glass.

"And when you saw how upset I was that night you told me it was nothing. You didn't think I'd be happy to hear you'd faced a moment of fear and realized you wanted to be with me?"

"I didn't want to spook you! I've been walking on eggshells not wanting to scare you off. I didn't tell you because I wanted to be with you." He shot up and began to pace.

"You lied to me and it's my fault?" She stood up but he pushed her back into her chair.

"Eat, damn you. You can be furious with me *and* eat some food."

"You can't tell me what to do, Marc Chase," she grumbled but forked up another bite of fish and some rice.

"You talk too much," he murmured more because he wanted to poke at her than because he thought so. "It *is* your fault partially. No, sit your pretty ass down. What I mean is that worrying about your reaction to things made me pull punches when I should have just shared. I see how that upset you and made you feel like I wasn't being honest. I was about what really mattered but you're right, honesty is important. But you haven't been totally honest with me either."

"About what?"

"Your doubts. Not the ones at the beginning but your feelings that there was something else and you kept quiet because you didn't want to rock the boat. Is that what you think? That my love for you is so thin that a question would break us up? I'm here, begging you to take me back. Is that what happens with a man who's so shallow he'd break up over a question?"

"And am I so fragile I can't bear hearing the truth?"

"Touché, sugar. So where do we go from here?"

"I don't know. Marc, I love you but at long last I've figured out a few things. I need love from a man who's worthy of me. And I need him to trust me enough to share all of himself and be honest. Even if he thinks I may not handle what he has to say well. There's got to be trust that the love is strong enough to bear the bumps."

He sighed. "Okay. That's fair. Here's what I propose because you and I are at a stalemate. I can tell you I'm that man and that I'll change and be totally honest from now on but it's clear words alone won't be enough. So let's try this. Give me today and tomorrow. Walls totally down. Complete honesty from each of us. If, when we wake up Sunday morning you don't believe I'm the right man, I'll leave you alone and let you move on."

His heart raced as she remained quiet, finishing up her dinner and mowing through the cheesecake.

He wanted to groan at the sight of her licking the tines of the fork when she'd polished off the last of the cheesecake but relief came when she nodded.

"All right, you have a deal."

Moving to her, he grabbed her wrist and pulled her up against his body. "Well then, if you're finished eating your way though Atlanta, let's get started."

Her gaze met his and he fell in, leapt into her with open arms because she meant everything to him and he wanted her to know it. He sensed her hesitation but she straightened her spine and opened her gaze. The shadows fell away and he saw her fear, her uncertainty and more importantly, her love.

Licking her lips, she exhaled and cleared her throat. "I worry that what you're really attracted to is the novelty. You know, the woman who didn't fall into your bed, thighs wide and begging you to fuck her. The woman who walked away first. Knowing you felt that bit of temptation but realized what we had was bigger, more than what you were giving up, means something to me."

Touched that she'd shared something so intimate, he gave in and kissed each eyelid before replying. "I love you, Liv. Enough that it's changed me in so many important ways. That day with Nancy, the one I didn't tell you about, it wasn't even that I *was* tempted. The fact is I haven't been tempted by anyone else but you since before I kissed you in April. It was just a moment when I realized that it was us. You and me. And it was forever. You weren't a passing fancy or a novelty. And you did so beg me to fuck you."

She grinned. "You're bad."

"I am. You make me that way."

She snorted. "You were born that way."

"Okay, partially. But you're the key. You unlocked part of me I didn't realize existed until you came along. I never ordered a woman to hold her thighs open while I went down on her or I'd stop. You make me crave pushing you in bed, seeing what your limits are."

"That was pretty hot. I can tell you if any other man had said the same thing to me I'd have held his head with my thighs until he suffocated."

Throwing his head back, he laughed. "There's no one like you, Olivia Davis." And there wasn't.

Need rushed through him. Need to be with her, to share intimacy, to touch and taste her in ways no other man would again. The need to re-establish their bond and connection.

Chapter Thirteen

If he didn't start the sexin', and soon, she'd wither and die. Liv needed him so badly she'd be begging him within moments.

He touched her. Deeply and with a rawness that was both intimate and scary. She wanted these two days to be real, to see the truth of his commitment because she meant what she said. She'd move on with her life because she'd wasted enough time on the wrong men for the wrong reasons.

But she wanted this man. Younger or not, he was the man of her dreams. And she wanted to dare imagining forever with him. But first, she wanted him to fuck her six ways 'til Sunday.

Arching her upper body away from him, she writhed until she got her long-sleeved shirt up and off, tossing it behind her.

"Oh. Well now." His cocky grin made things inside her tingle and then tighten. "It's like that is it?" His shirt followed and in three quick movements her bra was gone. He crushed his upper body to hers, skin to skin. The pleasure shot through her and out her mouth as a groan. Her nipples were diamond-hard, throbbing in time with her clit.

"You feel unbelievably good. I've missed this. I slept every night hugging my pillow but it wasn't the same." Liv's emotion thickened her words but she knew he needed to hear them as much as she needed to say them.

"Girl, I love you. No one ever said anything like that to me before. It disarms me," he murmured against her temple as he pressed hot kisses down her face, over the edge of her jaw to her mouth.

When he finally kissed her, after over a week of absence, she came home, felt the shape and form of a future she'd dared not imagine. His lips covered hers. No gentleness, only barely leashed passion as she opened to him in a gasp and his tongue barged in, taking what was his, had been his for months. He possessed her mouth, ate at it, devoured her, nibbled, licked, nipped and sucked.

Heat shot through her as his tongue flicked against hers, seductive. She'd missed his taste, the way his mouth felt against her own like he was made to be there.

Frissons of heat and pleasure flickered, sparking as his fingertips played at the small of her back, tracing over the indentations on either side of her spine and then along the top of her pants around to her belly button. She groaned as shivers of delight racked her body. He wrecked her, utterly. Small touches and caresses reached into her heart and captured it.

She swallowed his moan when her thumbs played over his collarbone, down the lightly haired chest to his nipples. He arched into her when she scored his nipples lightly with her fingernails and came back to flick her thumbs over them back and forth.

A slight roll of his hips and his cock pressed, hot and hard, against her body. Needing him with great intensity, her hands traced down each ridge of his abdomen and upon reaching his jeans, jerked them open.

One hand at the back of her head, holding her to the kiss, he yanked his jeans off. She heard the dual clunk of his boots and felt the breeze of movement when he threw the jeans over her shoulder. Quick, clever hands shoved her yoga pants down and she stepped out of them, kicking them away. Impatiently, he yanked her panties off. They stood pressed together a few moments, still.

He backed her toward the corner of the room where the small couch stopped her movement.

His mouth left hers and cruised down the column of her throat, across the sensitive skin of her collarbone and down to her nipples. First one and then the other.

With a frustrated sound, one handed he pressed her breasts together and bent to them, using mouth, teeth and tongue to pay them so much attention she felt orgasm began to build.

Reaching around his body, she grabbed his cock in a sure grip and pumped a fist around him. He thrust hard and the wetness from his pre-come slicked her grip.

Impatient to feel him inside her, she angled him, hiking her thigh around his hip.

"Shit!" He looked into her eyes as he thrust into her waiting heat, naked. His chest heaved. "Oh, sugar, that's so good. No. No don't move. If you move I'm going to come and I'm not wearing a condom."

Taking a deep breath and leaping into the void, hoping like hell he caught her, she writhed provocatively against him and watched as beads of sweat popped out on his forehead. "We're tested, I'm on the pill. If this is forever, make it forever."

"Are you sure?" She saw the toll of his self-control while he made sure she was really okay with it.

Nodding, she tightened her inner muscles around him.

"Damn! That felt good with a condom on, without it you're going to make me come in three seconds. This is a gift, Liv.

Thank you." Drawing out of her body nearly completely, he slowly pushed back in, setting a slow, deep rhythm. "Back, let's get you against that wall behind you."

He helped her hop backwards to the wall where she leaned back for purchase while he resumed his pace.

"Your pussy feels so hot and tight. I'm going to have you so many times it'll burn anyone else out of your brain out your body."

One of his hands cradled her ass while the other did naughty things to her nipple.

"Marc," she let a sob come, "there hasn't been anyone else since you kissed me the first time." Tears rolled down her face and he kissed them away.

"You wreck me. I adore you, everything about you, the good, the bad and the complicated. You're the most beautiful creature I've ever clapped eyes on."

This only made her cry harder as he continued to make love to her. It wasn't gentle or soft, it was unrestrained need unleashed and she felt like a goddess for edging away his control.

One of his hands moved to cup her throat gently, his thumb tracing back and forth over the skin beneath her jaw.

The length of his cock stroked over her clit each time he thrust into her pussy, sending ribbons of hot sensation through her, drawing her closer and closer to orgasm.

"Open your eyes, Liv. I want to see that moment when they blur and I lose you just a bit when you come. You're close, I can feel your pussy flutter around me. It's so good."

She dragged her eyes open and met his gaze, snared, helpless to do anything but feel as he stroked her closer and closer, the pleasure growing sharper and sharper with each moment.

Her breath grew shallow and suddenly it swallowed her whole, the wave of climax that had been building. Mouth open on a hoarse gasp of his name, her gaze was still locked with his even as her vision blurred a bit and she fell away, letting the rush of endorphins sweep her up and ride her.

Moments later, she blinked and found him smiling at her. "Beautiful. Now me." His fingers dug into the muscle and flesh of her ass as he pressed hard and deep and came, his gaze still with hers.

The depth of connection, of intimacy at staring into his eyes as he came clutched deep, pulled at her, tied her to him in ways she hadn't imagined. Seeing him in a moment of emotional and physical vulnerability and having him give it to her freely, swelled her heart as she loved him more than she thought possible.

Breaking their gaze, he dropped his head to her shoulder as he caught his breath for a few moments.

"Right. This is pretty swanky hotel. Is the bathtub big enough for two?"

She laughed. "I don't know. I hadn't thought about it. Let's go see."

જ્જાજ્ર

Marc went back out into the living room to grab the wine. He'd never experienced a sexual interlude so intimate before, not even with Liv. She gave him everything without holding back.

And being naked inside her had been earth-shattering. He'd never been inside a woman without a condom before and her trust in him, in giving him such a gift, was unsettling. But in a good way.

He realized she was serious about letting the walls down and he had to give it back to her in equal parts. He knew how to seduce her body but he had to remember part of this was in showing her he loved every part of her, not just the sex part.

Grinning, he picked up the phone and called the concierge desk.

She looked up at him from her perch in the rather large tub, naked and glistening. He honestly thought his brother Matt was the biggest idiot ever breathing to let this woman go.

He handed her a glass of wine and put his next to the tub as he climbed in behind her and pulled her back to his chest. "How you could have not seen this bathtub as a sex spectacular is beyond me."

"I wasn't thinking of sex when I came here."

"I'm sorry. I'm sorry that my not telling you about the Nancy thing led to all this complication."

"I'm sorry you felt like you had to walk on eggshells, Marc."

"That wasn't entirely fair of me to use that. Yes, I did feel hesitant about sharing it for the reasons I told you but I can't argue that you didn't have reasons not to be wary. I'd just worked so hard to prove I was genuinely in love with you, I didn't want to give you any reason to doubt that."

She turned and wrapped her thighs around him, pulling close.

"This is nice. You're very limber. I admire that in a woman."

Laughing, she took a sip of her wine before setting it on the side of the tub. "I'm going to have a *Come To Jesus* talk with Nancy when I get back to Petal."

Marc chuckled. "You won't be the first. Cassie got hold of her first, then Maggie, I think Matt and Kyle too. Oh and my momma."

Liv winced. "I almost feel sorry for her for that. Almost."

"Don't. She thought she'd *test* my commitment to you. She's sorry but it's not enough."

Liv grinned and leaned in to kiss his chin.

"What was that for?"

"You didn't take her side."

He laughed at that outright. "Do I look crazy? Sugar, she nearly broke us up because she acted like a selfish bitch. Her being sorry doesn't erase that. I almost lost the best thing that ever happened to me. I nearly kicked her butt myself."

"Hmpf."

"I like this side of you."

"The side where my goodies are?"

Lord how she made him laugh. "Well, that too. But I meant the possessive, slightly feral side. Not that you have anything to worry about. You don't. Liv, I'd never cheat on you. In the first place, I love you. In the second, I have honor."

"Well, I have to deal with an awful lot of female attention your way. Which sucks. I mean, it was bad with Matt but you're worse. You're a very flirty man. Women, some women, tend to purposely misunderstand that and take it for an invitation. I don't like it but I don't think you're fixin' to cheat on me. Let me just tell you, a knee in the junk is the least that'll happen to you if you really do cheat on me."

He winced but couldn't deny the viciousness in her eyes was a turn on. Man he was sick.

"Liv, sugar, I'm going to make a real effort not to be so flirty with other women. I don't want you being bothered by it and I don't want you to feel disrespected, nor do I want to send the wrong signals. It's something I do on auto-pilot. This is all sort of new to me, the being hopelessly in love with the most beautiful woman in the world thing. I'm learning as I go."

"I don't want you to give up who you are."

"You think flirting with women is who I am?"

She rolled her eyes. "No. But I don't want to change you. I just want to try and find a way we can be together without either one of us having to give up who we are."

He soaped a washcloth and began to minister to her, enjoying the way she arched into his touch like a cat.

"Olivia, woman, you are exasperating sometimes. Just when I think you're doing one thing, you go and do or say something that shows me just how unselfish and giving you are. You have such a tough exterior and it's all bullshit. You're a marshmallow, aren't you?"

"I am not. I am a hard assed bitch. Ask anyone."

He pushed her back playfully and she ducked under the water and got to her knees to return the favor and soap him up.

"I have asked and that's not anyone's impression of you at all. Well, except the mayor and that's good. He should be scared of you. Maybe his crush on you will wear off. I have to deal with male attention your way too, you know."

He watched as she stood and grabbed a towel before stepping out. "He's just lonely, that's all. And I don't come equipped with a harem but if you see me flirting or you feel uncomfortable about the way I interact with anyone, please tell me. I'd hate for you to feel bad."

Standing, he got her wet again as he embraced her.

A knock sounded on the door and he held a hand out. "I'll be right back."

"What are you up to?" she called out.

"Hold your horses."

She got dressed in the bedroom and peeked out to see what he was up to.

"Nosy. Come on out and bring a blanket."

"What?" She grabbed a blanket and skipped toward him.

He caught her, laughing, picking her up and she wrapped her legs around him. "Now that's the kind of leg wrapping I approve of."

He kissed her quickly and put her down on the couch.

"I had them bring up some DVDs and some snacks."

"You did?"

"Yeah. The Matrix movies and those weird chocolate things with the white stuff you like."

"Snowcaps? Where? Gimme!"

He put in the first movie and came back to the couch, handed her the box of candy and settled in beside her.

"You remembered I liked Snowcaps. That's one of the sweetest things anyone has ever done."

"It's candy, sugar, while I'm content to hog up credit that'll get me laid later, it's not that big a deal." Smiling, he put his arm around her shoulder and tucked the blanket around them both.

But it was a big deal. He noticed something small and seemingly inconsequential. They'd only gone to the movies once and she'd gotten the candy there. And the movies he'd gone to the trouble to get? She had just a teeny celebrity crush on Keanu Reeves.

The sex had blown her mind but the movies and the chocolate had shown her he'd noticed more about her than her bra size. It occurred to her she needed to be more mindful of what he liked too. She hadn't been as aware of things as she should have been, or at least she hadn't shown him. If they were to make a go of their relationship it was up to her to do her part as well.

As she snuggled into his side, she let hope settle into her bones. Hope that just maybe, Marc was more than her future, *they* were the future.

ಬಿ෩෩ೞ

Breathing heavily, Marc rolled off Liv's sleep-warm body and onto his back beside her. With a feline smile, she stretched, leaning over to kiss his chest over his heart.

"That was a very inspired good morning, Marc Chase."

"What can I say? You inspire me," he gasped out.

"Don't you need to get back to your clients? I feel bad that you're here when you have a business to run."

"You're more important to me than that. I couldn't have waited until tomorrow for you to come back to town. I wanted you to know I didn't betray you, wanted you to know how much I love you. One of my buddies from my old gym has taken my clients until Monday so that's not a problem." He cocked his head. "But thank you for asking, for thinking of it."

"I love you. Your business is important to you so it's important to me. Now get up. We're going to breakfast and then I have somewhere I'd like to take you."

They quickly got up and dressed and headed out, hand in hand. She drove him out of the city center, to a greasy spoon the likes of which she'd rarely seen anywhere else. But an older hippie couple owned and ran it so she knew firsthand they had healthy offerings too. When her mother had been in the hospice during those last seven months, she often snuck away to come to this place to get away from the pain and death. Every time she came to Atlanta in the twenty years since, she'd stopped in and it had become a part of her in a sense. A refuge.

He gave her a skeptical look when she pulled in.

"Stop. Trust me."

He took her hand and they walked in together. "I do. With all my heart if not my cholesterol."

"Livvie! How are you darlin'?"

"I'm well, Rain. And you?" Liv kissed the cheek of the bird thin woman with short, white hair.

"Pretty darned good. And who is this fine looking specimen?"

"This is my boyfriend, ugh, that's such a weird term for an adult woman to use, anyway, this is Marc Chase. Marc, this is Rain Scott. She and her husband Pete own this place."

Smiling and turning on the charm, Marc shook her hand.

"Boyfriend huh? That's nice to hear. Well let's get you to a table. Coffee will be up in a moment." Rain handed them menus and they sat near the windows overlooking a side vegetable garden.

Liv watched him through her lashes as he opened up his menu and his face changed.

"Sneaky." He grinned her way.

She shrugged. "I knew you'd like it. The food here is really good."

"And healthy. Thank you."

"I like to eat healthy too, you know."

He took her hand and kissed her knuckles. "I like you. How did you find this place? It's sort of off the beaten path."

She told him and noted that he was touched.

After breakfast, she took him to the cemetery. "I know this is sort of weird but when I'm here in Atlanta, I come by. My dad buried her here. The hospice she spent the last year of her life in is just across the way. She'd look out the window at these big oak trees and say that's where she wanted to rest. I don't think he ever denied her anything. I wish she was in Petal but he's bought the plot next to hers and my sister lives here now anyway." She got quiet, looking off into the distance.

Marc stopped and stared at her, turning her chin so she faced him. "I don't know what to say. I'm amazed that you'd share this with me."

"You are? Have I been so selfish with you?"

Marc felt the gulf between them again but determined to push through it. "No. It's not that. But you've kept a lot of stuff to yourself. I guess I'm just seeing how much I didn't see, didn't know."

"Okay. That's fair I guess."

Her shoulders dropped and he felt like an asshole. He hadn't meant to make her feel bad. In fact, he was touched she'd brought him there. But she hadn't talked about her mom much before and he realized there was so much he didn't know about her.

"Liv, I'm sorry. I didn't want to make you feel guilty or lacking."

"You feel how you feel."

He sighed. "Eggshells here, Liv. I'm just expressing my surprise. I want to be able to be honest with you but I'm going to hold back if I hurt you."

"I don't want to do this here. Let's go."

He stopped her, grabbing her hand. "Honey, this is going to be a work in progress. You know that. We can't make things right if you just give up. First things first. I'm honored, truly, that you'd share this with me. Let's go and visit your mother and then we can talk." He tried to show her how much he loved her, wanted her to see it in his eyes.

Keeping her hand in his, he followed her across the quiet grass to the flat, pale stone. They knelt together and he nearly gasped when he saw the name. He *knew* it was her mother but seeing Olivia's name on a headstone gave him a start.

"I know. It's odd isn't it? My father told me shortly after my mother died, that it was hard for him to come here because he thought of me every time."

Her voice was quiet, soft and he put his arm around her shoulder.

"She was only thirty-five when she died. So young." A shiver ran through him again at the comparison.

"I'm now older than she was when she died. She passed two days after her birthday. And yet she had two children and a marriage when she died. I have none of that."

He remained quiet. Not because he didn't have something to say about that but because her mother's grave wasn't the place to say it.

"Lilacs and lilies. Pretty." He indicated the flowers there.

"My sister is most likely the source of the lilies. I brought the lilacs. They're out of season but I know this little florist not too far away and I call ahead and he orders them for me. My mom loved them. She wanted to name my sister Lilac." Liv laughed. "I know. Well, Susan lucked out I think."

"She was the year behind me in school so I don't know her very well. Not well enough to really get a feeling about whether she'd be a Lilac or not. But she doesn't seem like one." In truth, Liv's sister had been pretty wild back in the day. They hadn't run in the same circles but she'd gotten around quite a bit, partied pretty hard, got into trouble.

They stood and walked back to the car, driving back to the hotel quietly. He realized just how complicated his woman was. She was so confident on the outside but each layer he uncovered showed him a wounded heart. It began to settle in that this issue between them was bigger than the Nancy thing. He was also pretty sure Liv herself hadn't realized it just yet. He'd have to confront it and make her see it. It wouldn't be easy, he had the feeling there'd be more tears before the breakthrough, but he needed to be steadfast so they could build their future. He meant to have her as his wife and the mother of his children and that meant she had to accept he wasn't going anywhere.

She spoke then, pulling him out of his thoughts. He looked at her as she walked through the room, the grief on her face.

"She's not. A Lilac, I mean. She's had a lot of problems but in the last few years she's straightened herself out. I suppose you know that, as you two were in school together the way you were. Getting away from Petal was good for her. She's here in Atlanta now. Got married two years ago, has two kids."

She sat on the couch and put her feet up.

"You're not close." It was hard for him to imagine not being close to a sibling.

"We are in our own way. Susan was young when our mom died. Seven. It was harder on her because pretty much all of her memories of our mother were of her being sick. I had her for longer, it affected me differently. And I had Maggie. By that point neither one of us had a mother. Hers wasn't dead but may as well have been for all the attention Maggie ever got from her. My dad sort of checked out. Gave up expending emotion. He never neglected us, we had a nice place to live, he came to our plays and school stuff. But when he moved to Florida ten years ago, it wasn't like there was much of a difference in my life. He's happier now I think because the memories are farther away."

"I'm sorry. I can't imagine not being close to my family. But I'm glad you and Maggie had each other." And he began to understand her more with each bit of her life she exposed. "So, why haven't you shared any of this before now?"

She sighed heavily. "Marc, it's not like I was hiding it. But I don't just take my dates out to the cemetery ninety minutes away to show them my mother's grave. I've never shown anyone her grave. It doesn't matter, she's been dead over twenty years. I shouldn't have taken you today, it was a stupid impulse."

"What? Stupid? For you to open up to me? Is that what you think? Sharing with me is stupid?"

"Oh get off your fucking self-righteous high horse, Marc. Here's a clue, I'm not perfect. And here's another, neither are you. I don't come from some perfect, *Leave It To Beaver* life. My mom didn't greet me at the door with cookies when I got home from school. My sister was a drunk by fifteen and my mother died when I was thirteen. I don't have family dinners every Sunday and hang out with my family on purpose."

"Stop it. I'm on to you, Liv. You get all bitchy when people get close to keep 'em back. It's not going to happen with me. I'm in this with you for the long haul. And yes, you do have family dinners every Sunday. With my family, who are now your family. And you're going to have to deal with that. You can get close to people, Liv."

She winced and he knew he'd hit home on that one. "Oh man, is this going to get all *Oprah*?"

He knew her game and didn't let her get to him. It was all a front.

"You can't love on your terms, you know. That's not how it works. Love, real love makes demands. You have to give, compromise. You have to let yourself be vulnerable."

"Oh man. And what about you? Mr. perfect family and well adjusted emotions, what do you have to give up? Your pussy buffet? If you're so fabulous why've you been fucking your way through every female in town for years?"

He waved that away. "Sharp tongued bitch. You don't scare me, Liv. I've seen your underbelly. And I love you anyway. Do you hear that? I love you. I'm not leaving. Stop it. Let it all go because I'm not going to walk out that door because you're not perfect. And death isn't desertion. She couldn't help it and you didn't give her cancer. Your father was weak but he's human. You survived and you're a strong woman worthy of love and respect. I love you. Maggie loves you. That baby adores you, Liv. He lights up when he hears your voice. My family loves you. Your friends love you."

Tears ran down her face as she stood and began to pace. He watched her from his chair, wanting to go to her but realizing they needed to play this out until she let it all go. This was the issue, not his omission of the thing with Nancy, not his flirting, not his former skirt chasing ways. Those things were part of it, yes, but it was her flat out terror that everyone she loved she would lose because she wasn't worthy. That was a huge burden for one person to carry and he planned to knock it off her shoulders, even if he made her cry to do so.

"I'm not a charity case, Marc. Is that it? The novelty of fixing me?"

"You'd like to think so. That way you could blow off what's between us and continue to hold yourself back or keep hooking up with men you can control and never commit to fully." He shrugged. "You can't control me, Liv. I'm your equal. Snuck in there, didn't I? I didn't quite get that until I was way too far gone in love with you. I suppose I have my own share of emotional shit to shovel."

Her hair stuck up from the way she kept running her hands through it and tugging at it. She looked like a pretty porcupine. It made him smile and she made a distressed sound. "What? What are you smiling at, Dr. Phil?"

He chuckled. "I love your sense of humor. I was smiling because I like looking at you. You're cranky when you're on the ropes."

"Oh man, now you're going to be patronizing on top of judgmental and self righteous?"

"I'm not judgmental, Liv. I'm in no position to judge you, even if I wanted to. And I'm not self righteous. I understand you. Drives you nuts too. We're going to fight you know. It's part of who we are. But fighting won't change how much I love you. You can blow your top and throw a tantrum and I'm still going to love you." His father's advice some months back really hit home, then.

"Matt and I never fought."

"Yeah, and that turned out well, didn't it?" Ruthlessly, he had to push past his need to soothe her to keep going. "Come on, Liv. Putting Matt between us isn't going to work. He doesn't want to be there, first of all. Which is his mistake because losing you has to be the most asinine thing he's ever done and believe me, I've known him my whole life and he's done a lot of asinine things. And secondly, I'm not threatened. What you and I have is *real*. It's messy and complicated and frustrating, but that's what love is. You fucked my brother for a while. And the fact that he didn't love you isn't about you being lacking. It's about his own shit and your total incompatibility outside of bed. You're a rock star in bed, Liv. I know you know that. But so what? It's not everything and you know it. So after a while, people fall away because you can't live on fucking alone. Brody is a douche bag and never was good enough for you and all the others have been the same. But I'm not them and you can't hide from that."

She stared at him, openmouthed, and he leaned back in his chair. "You can't work me, Liv. I know you're a bitch, I know you're cranky, I know you're loving, I know you're smart and funny, I know you're giving and generous. I'm not walking off because you're not flawless. I don't want a diamond, I want a wife." He smiled when she paled.

The man was infuriating! Liv snorted and resumed pacing. "You don't want a wife, Marc."

"Yes I do. I want you to marry me. Normally, I'd ask you on Christmas, it's a family tradition you know. But instead I'm asking you right now. We can get married on Christmas instead. Yeah, the more I think about it, the better it sounds. What do you say?"

"You're asking me to marry you in the middle of a fight? Are you out of your mind?" Her heart thundered as hope warred with terror.

"Liv, I lost my mind when I kissed you on Founder's Day. We've established that already. That night when I first touched your lips I knew. I fought it for a while but it was useless so I gave in. And I didn't want to resist you any more anyway. It's funny but I don't think I truly knew just how much I loved you until today when you took me to your momma's grave. Because not only did you share that with me but it opened up that last barrier, the big one. People you love leave you."

Grief, rage, fear and the ember of hope he'd stoked burst through her and a sob tore from her lips. "You don't know anything!" But he did. Damn it, he did. How is it that he did and she didn't?

Is this what people meant when they referred to a moment of clarity? Everything fell away then as she stood, weeping, letting it all rush through her. Jesus. He was right. Maggie was in her heart because they'd been friends before she lost her mother and how could she not love Nicholas when he came from the sister of her heart? But even Cassie and Dee she'd kept from loving fully. Matt, sweet wonderful Matt had never been right for her but he hadn't been a challenge to be with. In the end she'd left because she knew he'd never love her but holy crap, she'd never really loved him either, not totally. She'd thought she had but as she compared it to the way she felt for Marc, it was a shallow, pale thing.

How is it that she never really confronted this? How could she not have known? She knew she had a basic fear when people around her got sick but this was huge. Man, like self help book huge. And Marc saw it. He saw it and he confronted it and he fought it. For her.

Dimly, she realized she'd slid to the floor and he'd moved closer, his hand on her thigh. "Let it go, baby. I'm not going to leave you. I love you. I adore you. You're worth everything, don't you see that? I didn't leave you. I came after you. I will always work for you, for us. Because, Liv, that's what real love is. I can't guarantee I won't die." She caught his shrug through the veil of her tears. "That's beyond my ability to promise. But I'm a healthy guy, I work out, I eat right, I wear sunscreen and I want decades of happiness with you. All things that are in my favor long life wise. And being with you will keep my mind sharp because you're a pain in the ass. A beautiful pain in the ass and worth it, but crotchety, cranky, defended, defensive and sulky sometimes too."

"Is that supposed to be flattery?"

"Nope." He kissed her forehead and pressed some tissues into her hands. "It's honesty."

In a rush, she threw her arms around him, clutching him tight. "I love you so much, Marc."

He stood, still holding her tight. "And I love you, Liv. You gonna make an honest man out of me? You haven't said anything about my proposal. I don't have a ring. I've been looking but I planned on asking you in a few months at Christmas. We'll get right on that. Well, after we have sex, because that's necessary."

"Sex first." Fear still lived in her heart, even as she tried to beat it back.

"Nope. I'm not some floozy who'll just sleep with any old gal. I need a promise of marriage first. For my honor and all."

She laughed and the fear loosened its hold. Taking a deep breath, she looked him in the eyes and defied the fear of losing him. "Okay. You can't dump me when I get old though. I forbid it. You made your bed by marrying an older woman."

"Deal. Wow, you've made me a very happy man." He started walking toward the bedroom.

"You saw it all, Marc. You saw inside me, past the bullshit and you loved me anyway." She started crying again.

"Because you're the best thing that's ever happened to me. And you know my flaws too. Yeah I did fuck my way through every woman in town. I do have some issues about living in the shadow of the Chase men. Trying to act like it doesn't matter so I never really treated myself like I mattered. Not emotionally anyway. You knew that about me and you loved me anyway. How lucky am I?"

"Not as lucky as you're going to get in a few minutes."

Marc sat back on the bed and looked her up and down. "Absolutely the most beautiful woman I've ever seen. Inside and out. Take your clothes off for me, sugar."

She toed off her shoes and socks and then stood straight, her gaze on him. Sliding her hands up her torso, she smiled when his eyes widened as she paused to trail her fingertips over her nipples. Slowly, she slid each button loose until the front of her sweater was open and she let it drop.

"I love that bra. You need a dozen more."

A quick flick and she popped the catch between her breasts and let the bra follow the blouse.

"Now, I don't normally get crass in the presence of such a fine lady and all, but your tits are fabulous."

She chuckled and traced the nipples, round and round until her breath hitched and his eyes widened, glued to her movement.

"Hoo boy, that's hot." His hands convulsed a few times on his thighs like he wanted to touch her.

Catching her bottom lip between her teeth, she moved her hands to her jeans, lowering the zipper and bending forward to pull them off.

She turned to grab a chair and moved it to the foot of the bed. A quick yank on each side of her panties and the ties loosed and they fell away, leaving her totally naked.

In for a penny. She sat, hooking a leg up on the arm of the chair. His aroused groan emboldened her and she met his gaze.

"Go on then, sugar. Show me how you like to be touched."

"First, take your clothes off. I want you to have your cock handy."

He took a slow breath and got to his knees to get rid of the sweater and then shimmied out of jeans, socks and underwear. Reclining, he put some pillows behind his back and raised an eyebrow at her. "Your move."

Liv couldn't believe she was going to do this in front of him but she felt so sexy she couldn't stop. He made her feel wanton and she liked that a lot.

Wetting a fingertip with her tongue, she moved back to her nipples pinching and rolling them until her breathing grew shallow and she felt her pussy slicken in response.

"Touch your pussy, Liv. I can see how wet you are. I want you to know while you're doing it that my tongue will be there later on. I'm going to eat you until you can't come any more. Over and over again. I love your taste."

Wow. Her entire body tightened at that. She knew he'd do it too. And boy did she look forward to it.

One hand slid down her belly, her fingertips lightly grazing her labia, teasing them both until she could no longer stand it. She slid her fingers into the wet flesh, finding her clit swollen. Without even meaning to, her hips lurched forward when she touched it. She wouldn't be long, she wanted him too much and was already very close.

He crawled off the bed and knelt on the floor between her thighs. "Keep going. I just wanted a better view." He laid his head on her thigh and reached out to hold her wide open.

She was too far along to be shy so she covered her clit with her thumb and slid two fingers deep. Both of them moaned softly as she began to roll her hips.

Closer and closer, her clit hardened and her pussy grew wetter, hotter. He blew over that humid flesh and she cried out, sliding her thumb back and forth over her clit as she climaxed.

The muscles in her body were still jumping when she found herself picked up and dropped into his lap, pussy sliding down onto his cock as he'd sat where she had in the chair.

"I know I said I'd go down on you, and I will soon. But I had to be inside you right this minute. I've never in my life seen anything sexier. I'm so damned close I thought I'd come while I watched you. But I'd rather come inside you. Just an appetizer to take the edge off. Ride me, sugar."

Squeezing her knees between the outside of his thighs and the chair, she rose and fell on him. Electric pleasure arced up her spine each time he filled her fully. Her hands rested on his chest for balance and his roved her body, played with her nipples, kneaded her thighs and shoulders, caressed her face and ran through her hair.

She tightened herself around him, adding a swivel each time she took him into her completely. She knew he wasn't lying when he said he was almost there, his thighs trembled. Satisfaction that he'd been so aroused by her so completely roared through her.

Bending to him, she kissed his upturned lips. "I love you, Marc. For seeing all of me and loving me anyway." She increased her speed. "And for saying I was a rock star in bed."

His laugh died into a gasp of her name as she felt him come, his fingers tightening on her hips just this side of pain.

Standing, he took them both to the bed and they collapsed in a heap. "I can't do anything else but love you, Liv. I was meant to do it. Born to."

Chapter Fourteen

Liv and Marc walked into the Chases' front foyer the next evening. They hadn't told anyone they were back and they'd had a few errands so they'd returned from Atlanta the day before to finish them.

Polly came around the corner, distracted, reading glasses perched on her nose. She stopped when she caught sight of them both. "Oh! You're back. Honey, welcome back." She rushed to Liv and hugged her tight.

"Thank you. It's okay that I'm here?"

Polly frowned a moment. "I can't believe you'd ask that. Of course. It's more than okay. You're supposed to be here. It's Sunday night and that's family dinner and you're family." She grinned at Marc. "I'm going to go add two more places to the table. Go on through, everyone's in the living room."

Marc winked at Liv as they walked back and into the room where the rest of the family had gathered.

Maggie called out a pleased hello and Liv was engulfed by hugs from Shane, Kyle, Edward, Matt and Cassie. Nicholas made piercing cries, demanding her attention and she got to all fours next to where he'd rolled over and pushed himself up on his blanket.

"Dude, you're an amazing little genius aren't you? Rolling over and pushing up! Pretty soon it'll be eating your first Cheerio and sitting up. Then college."

He grinned at her as he lost his balance and rolled back over. Sitting up, she picked him up and rained kisses all over his face.

"I think I'm jealous," Marc said as he dropped a kiss on the top of Nicholas' head. "She likes you more than me, kid."

"Uh, Liv?" Maggie moved closer.

"Don't, not yet. Wait until Polly gets in here or there'll be hell to pay," Liv murmured.

Maggie just kissed her square on the mouth and grinned.

"Wait, can we see that again?" Matt said and Edward bopped him with a pillow.

"Lamb? I think you need to come on in here," Edward called out.

Polly click-clacked into the room and smiled at the sight. "What is it, Edward? The potatoes are done and I was getting ready to smash them."

"You were supposed to tell me so I could do it, Mom." Cassie frowned at her.

"Oh I was right there. But you can now." Polly laughed.

Liv handed Nicholas to his mother and let Marc pull her to standing.

"We have an announcement to make." Marc put his arm around her waist. "Liv and I are engaged."

Polly whooped so loud Nicholas began to cry but only for a moment as every adult within reach swooped in to kiss or comfort him. Assured he was the center of the universe again, he calmed down.

Polly hugged both Marc and Liv to her tight, followed by Edward and then everyone else.

"I can't believe I didn't even see that ring," Polly sniffled and looked at the pretty diamond engagement ring on Liv's left hand.

"We just got it this afternoon. I moved into Liv's house last night. Well mostly. I figured you all could help with the big stuff."

"Into our house you mean."

Marc smiled at Liv and she felt like a princess.

"When's the wedding?"

"Christmas Day. I know it's an odd day but I like the connection to tradition and I'll never forget our anniversary that way." Marc laughed.

"Christmas? That only gives us eight weeks!" Polly looked aghast.

"We want it simple, Momma. We'd like to do it here if that's okay with you. Just family, like we'd do anyway. We don't need catering except for the cake because we'd have dinner here as it is."

"Is it okay? Of course it's okay! My goodness, congratulations to you both. Olivia, welcome to the family, honey. And Marc, you've done well." Edward nodded at his son.

"I owe it to you, Dad. You raised me right and gave me some great advice."

"He did, did he? And what advice was that?" Liv grinned.

"To never share his advice with my fiancé."

ॐ౭ౘ౨

After dinner when the women were all chattering about wedding details, Marc sat with his brothers and his father, watching a football game.

"You chose well, son. I mean that. Olivia is a good woman. She'll be a fine wife and keep you on your toes."

"Thank you, Dad. I think so too. I hope you know I'll be coming to you for advice lots and lots."

Edward laughed. "Marc, I still go to my daddy for advice about your momma." He looked to Matt. "You're next. I had a dream about you last night."

Matt looked surprised. "Well is it going to be one of their exes? Because we sure do seem to find women for each other in this family."

"True. But I don't know who it'll be. I just saw cookies and not in a euphemistic sense. Actual cookies. Damned if I know what that means."

"Maybe Matt needs to hang out at The Honey Bear because his future wife is a baker." Shane laughed.

"Or a Girl Scout troop leader." Marc stood and stretched. "Well gentlemen, I have to take my fiancée home. She has to go back to work tomorrow, as do I. Shane, don't forget that we're upgrading your workout on Tuesday."

Liv met him in the hallway and for a moment there was nothing else but her face and the way she looked at him. She grinned and he laughed, grabbing her and jogging out the door into the night full of possibilities.

About the Author

To learn more about Lauren Dane, please visit www.laurendane.com. Send an email to Lauren at lauren@laurendane.com or stop by her messageboard to join in the fun with other readers as well. http://www.laurendane.com/messageboard

Look for these titles

Now Available

Giving Chase
Taking Chase

Coming Soon:

Making Chase
Reading Between the Lines

It was nothing personal, just a business arrangement.

Nothing Personal
© *2007 Jaci Burton*

Ryan McKay is a multi-millionaire with a problem. He needs a bride to fulfill the terms of his grandfather's will. Unfortunately, the one he chose just bailed on him and he's hours away from losing his company. Enter Faith Lewis—his demure, devoted assistant. Ryan convinces Faith to step in and marry him, assuring her their marriage is merely a business deal. Ryan is certain he can keep this strictly impersonal. After all, he's the product of a loveless marriage and for years has sealed his own heart in an icy stone. Despite Faith's warmth, compassion and allure, he's convinced he's immune to her charms.

Faith will do anything for her boss, but—marry him? The shy virgin sees herself as plain and unattractive, a product of a bitter mother who drummed into her head that she wasn't worthy of a man's love. But she agrees to help Ryan fulfill the terms of his grandfather's will, hoping she doesn't lose her heart to him in the process.

But love rarely listens to logic, and what follows is anything but business.

Available now in ebook from Samhain Publishing.

Darcy and Mac are "best friends with benefits", but now Mac wants more than just the hot sex. He wants Darcy forever. And he'll risk everything to get her.

The Boy Next Door
© 2007 Jessica Jarman

The last thing Darcy Phillips wants after the end of a disastrous relationship is to get involved with another man. Being free and unattached was the plan until her old pal Thomas "Mac" MacAllister strolls back into her life.

Mac has always loved Darcy but the timing was always wrong. Now, she's home and unattached. And after a night of wine and conversation, things turn hot fast. But Darcy isn't ready for more than the physical and she definitely doesn't want anyone knowing what the two of them are up to. Especially her mother.

It isn't long, though, before Mac wants more. Much more. Yet Darcy isn't sure she's willing to risk their long-time relationship for something as dangerous as love. But Mac is a man who knows what he wants and he's not afraid to go after it.

Using their incendiary passion as a starting point, Mac sets out to win the girl of his dreams and show her that everything she wants...is right next door.

Available now in ebook from Samhain Publishing.

Together they find a special love—can it survive the threat stalking her?

Giving Chase
© *2006 Lauren Dane*

Some small towns grow really good looking men! This is the case with the four Chase brothers. The home grown hotties are on the wishlist of every single woman in town and Maggie Wright is no exception.

Maggie has finally had it with the men she's been dating but a spilled plate of chili cheese fries drops Shane Chase right into her lap. The sheriff is hot stuff but was burned by a former fiancée and is quite happy to play the field.

After Shane's skittishness sends him out the door, Maggie realizes that Kyle Chase has had his eye on her from the start. Now that Shane has messed up, Kyle has no intention of letting anything stop him from wooing her right into his bed.

Despite Maggie's happiness and growing love with Kyle, a dark shadow threatens everything—she's got a stalker and he's not happy at all. In the end, Maggie will need her wits, strength and the love of her man to get her out alive.

Available now in ebook and print from Samhain Publishing.

GREAT
cheap
FUN

Discover eBooks!

THE FASTEST WAY TO GET THE HOTTEST NAMES

Get your favorite authors on your favorite reader, long before they're out in print! Ebooks from Samhain go wherever you go, and work with whatever you carry—Palm, PDF, Mobi, and more.

WWW.SAMHAINPUBLISHING.COM

CPSIA information can be obtained at www.ICGtesting.com
Printed in the USA
LVOW042214130812

294225LV00001B/69/A